Amity and the Angel

Damselfly Books 2017

Amity and the Angel

Sharon Griffiths

A CIP catalogue record for this book is available from the British Library.

ISBN-13: 978 154 7033502

ISBN-10: 154 7022507

Published in Great Britain

Damselfly Books

For Maeve, Bethan and Freddie.

May your lives always be full of music and stories.

Historical Note

After the Great Oil Wars of the 21st century the world lay in ruins. Oilfields burned out of control for decades. What hadn't been destroyed by warfare was choked by smoke. Thick oily smoke hung over the planet, choking seas, rivers and plants, making life almost impossible. Of those who survived the war most died of disease and starvation in a world reduced to wasteland. Technology was just about destroyed. The world had been set back thousands of years.

Yet, scattered far and wide, a few people survived, formed themselves into new communities and found ways of living in this new bleak world. One such was the Celtic Alliance in the far north and west of what used to be known as Britain.

Chapter 1

Otters

I clambered up the rock, my heavy skirt trailing in the puddles. At the top I curled my toes around the ridge, swaying for a second as I pulled myself upright against the swirling wind. The rocks were sharp under my feet, a patch of seaweed slithery under my toes and all I could hear was the boom of the waves pounding into the cove. But I'd seen the footprints in the sand. That was enough. I wasn't going to look. I wasn't going to check. That would be cheating, as though I didn't trust him. And I did, absolutely.

So, head back, arms flung wide, eyes open on the heavens, I sprang out into the vast unknown of the warm empty air. A heart-lurching glimpse of dizzy blue sky, the screech of startled birds and then I saw sand rushing up to meet me…

And I was in Fin's arms. As I knew I would be.

We fell onto the sand, rolling over and over so it trickled and tickled over our skin and stuck to our clothes.

'Did you look before you jumped?' asked Fin, his eyes laughing.

'No! Of course not!'

'And what if I hadn't been there to catch you?'

'Then I'd have landed on my own two feet. But I knew you'd be there.'

We lay close together, our faces inches apart. Gently, Fin tugged my headscarf off and my hair tumbled loose, spilling down onto the silvery sand. Fin gazed at it for a moment. 'I wasn't sure you'd be able to get away,' he said

'If there's not enough potatoes peeled for the village meal tonight then it's your fault,' I said. I hardly dared move as he reached up his hand and stroked my hair, his fingers twining in the strands. 'Bekah's going to have to peel twice as fast. I'm sure Mrs Chief Elder saw me sneaking out. She'll be watching out for me.'

'Let her!' crowed Fin. 'She's a dried up old busy body, only happy when she's stopping everyone else enjoying themselves. Well, she's not going to stop us!'

We lay in the sun, his arm around me, my head on his chest. Through his old football shirt I could feel his heart beat. I felt so close to him... Suddenly he sat up. 'Look! On the rock!'

'The otters! They're here again! There's four, no *five* of them. Oh Fin, it must be a good sign, mustn't it?'

'The sea's getting cleaner. There must be more fish. Maybe the world's getting back to normal.'

'Whatever normal is...'

We had to smile at the otters. The young ones scampered around the rocks, their coats sleek and shining. Then one at a time they slid into the water and vanished. We only heard the cry of the birds and

2

the splash and crash of the water as we looked at each other, uncertain of what would happen next.

'Race you to the top of otter rock!' said Fin. He sprang up and set out for the outcrop of tall rocks.

'Ha!' I yelled. 'You're not going to beat me!' And I tucked up my skirt and raced after him. He'd got a start on me but I was determined. Sand sprayed everywhere as we ran. He was first at the rocks but I took a different side from him and clambered up hand over hand, not caring if I scraped my skin, or slipped on the seaweed, or tore my stupid skirt. I was just determined to get there first.

Then just before he got to the top, Fin turned round. 'You won't catch me!' he shouted.

'Yes I will!' I flung myself on to the top a split second before him. 'I win!' We perched there laughing, hand in hand. Without its headscarf my hair blew everywhere, so I could hardly see. Even though it was cut regulation short, Fin's hair was still a mass of curls. The Elders hated his hair as if its very curls were immoral. They hated his Arsenal shirt too, in its bold bright red. But ever since he'd found it in a broken cupboard in an abandoned house, he'd worn it most days. He would say it was a link he didn't understand to a world he'd never known and just laughed when the Elders disapproved. 'It's just a *shirt*,' he'd say. 'It's not *evil*.'

Fin always laughed at the Elders. When the preachers are promising us hellfire and damnation everyone in church looks scared. Then I see Fin looking so solemn that I know inside he must be laughing. 'Don't you take *anything* seriously?'

'Lots of things, Amity. But nothing the Elders say, not those narrow minded old men who want to keep us trapped in the past.'

Out at sea, the rusty oil rigs looked like giant wading birds pecking hungrily at the carcases of platforms collapsed under the waves. Everyone knew they needed skilled workers and technology to repair them but our own Celtic Alliance was a long way from re-learning those skills.

Fin looked out at the rigs and my heart lurched as I knew what he was going to say. 'I'm going to the Engineers,' he said, still not looking at me. 'In Mainland. As soon as they can get a boat across. Your Davy's going too. They told us this morning.'

Fin and my favourite brother! The two people I cared most about in the world, leaving the island.

Like Fin, I stared out at sea. I didn't want to look at him. I didn't want to cry. He couldn't hide his pride and excitement. Only the brightest and best boys were chosen to go to Mainland and learn the skills needed to re-master technology.

'I just can't wait to get to Mainland.' His eyes gleamed. Then he took my hand, his face sad. 'I really wish you were coming too, Amity.'

'Not as much as I do!' I snatched my hand away and flung a pebble into the sea as hard as I could.

It was so unfair. Only the boys had the chance to go to Mainland. Only the boys got the chance to stay in school. I'd had to leave years before. 'I don't want to spend the rest of my life on the island just cooking and cleaning and having babies.' I said. 'There must be something more!' I flung another pebble hard to make the point, then jumped off the rock and went racing up the beach.

Fin caught up with me, grabbed my arm and pulled me down on the sand. He ran his fingers through my hair, stroked my face, wrapped himself around me so again I could feel his heart beating next to mine. 'It will change one day," he said fiercely. 'And if it doesn't then we'll have to be the ones to make it change.'

'How can we? What can we do, just the two of us?'

'Not sure. But we will. I'm going now but I'll come back for you,' he said, as he kissed my forehead. 'One day, Amity, we'll both get away from here. I promise you.' And he kissed my chin. 'We both know there's more to the world than here. And we'll find it together.' He paused. 'Here, I made you this,' he said, reaching into his jacket pocket and put something small and wooden in my palm.

I stared down at the tiny carved animal, polished to a silky smoothness. Its eyes glinted and its coat glistened.

'An otter! Fin, it's beautiful.'

'I made it for you, to remind you of this place and of our time here. When I go away you'll have it and know I'll come back.'

'I love it,' I said and put it to my lips. 'I'll keep it safe. But...'

Fin kissed my mouth and his lips tasted sweet and of the sea, of possibilities.

A few days later the ferry came from Mainland and Fin and Davy left the island. As we waved them goodbye, Bekah - who had always loved Davy - cried 'Oh, I shall miss him so much! I can't wait for them to come back!' I couldn't speak. I could hardly breathe. I clutched the tiny carved otter deep in my pocket and watched Fin and Davy march away.

Chapter 2

The Angel

An angel! An angel fallen to earth and swept in on the tide...

Well, that's what I thought when I saw him. He looked unearthly, beautiful, not from our world. He lay curled under the shelter of the rock where the otters play. The tide washed over his feet and his clothes were heavy with water, his eyes closed, his face bruised. But his hair... Even tangled with seaweed and salt it was long and golden and in the evening sun it gleamed against the rocks like a halo. Back then I'd never seen a man with such long hair. But I'd seen pictures of angels.

Pulling my dress up over my knees, I splashed through the surf, hardly noticing how icy it was or how the tug of the current pulled at me. I could see the angel was tall, even with his body bent around the rock. His skin, despite the paleness and the bruising glowed golden. And he had such beautiful long eyelashes...

6

Where had he come from? How had he got here? Not even islanders came to this beach very often. It meant sliding down an overgrown path and balancing on stepping stones through an icy stream. That's why Fin and I had always had it to ourselves.

My fingers curled around the tiny carved otter deep in my pocket. Two years now since Fin had gone.

A fierce wave crashed over the rocks. The angel stranger disappeared under the spray until the tide sucked back on itself with a rattle and pluck of pebbles and his golden hair shimmered under the surface.

Quickly I grabbed him under his shoulders and hauled him out of the water as if he were a stubborn calf or awkward sheep. One of his arms looked odd. The angle wasn't right. He must have broken it. Then he retched and a trickle of sea water dribbled out of his mouth.

Not an angel then.

But not dead either, though he soon would be if he stayed where he was. I dug my heels in, felt them sink deep into the wet sand and had to tug them free and then pull the angel past the rocks, up to where the sand was white and powdery. The tide wouldn't reach there tonight.

'Come on,' I muttered as I dragged him away from the waves, trying my best not to disturb his damaged arm. 'You've got out of the sea once. You're not going to give it another chance to get you, not if I can help it.'

For an angel he was very heavy. He groaned as I dragged him along.

'Sorry, no time to be gentle,' I shouted in his ear.

His head drooped and still he didn't open his eyes.

'You need help. No way I can carry you up to the village so I'm going to leave you here for a bit. Do you understand?'

He groaned and retched again. Maybe that meant yes. I moved him onto his good side so that he wouldn't choke, placing his damaged arm as gently as I could. I scooped the long hair off his face and out of his mouth. How smooth his skin was under my fingers. I tugged off my headscarf and folded it round a big pebble and jammed it under his head so that he wouldn't loll back and choke.

'There, that's the best I can do for a pillow and now I'm going to get help,' I touched his cheek. 'Don't worry, I'll be back soon.'

My dress was wet and covered with sand, slapping and stinging my bare legs as I ran along the beach, across the stepping stones, and up the narrow path, my knitting sheath, as always, bumping against my hip. It was almost dark. I'd already stayed out too long and was late. Father would be angry. But he would know what to do and organise help for the man like an angel.

It was a strange evening. After the storms and winds of the last few days everywhere was still, almost silent. On the Island we're well used to wild and windy weather. But that evening even the wind turbines were barely turning and it made me realise how accustomed we were to their low rumble as the sails turned. Now all I could hear was the slap and suck of the sea and the sheep chomping at the short grass that led up from the shoreline.

And hoof beats. Hoof beats? Yes, drumming along the sandy track to the village. A rare sound. Our

Dr John had a small sturdy pony but the few horses we had on the island were clumpy, plodding creatures, used only to pull a plough or a heavy cart. They could never gallop so light and so fast. Only members of The Elect had elegant horses to ride. These hoof beats meant someone very important was coming, Maybe it was something to do with the angel…

My heart thudding nearly as loud as the hooves. I dived into the shadows behind one of the polytunnels, the huge flapping greenhouses where we grew vegetables. To be caught out alone so late, in such a state with my hair uncovered would mean big trouble. I pressed as far back as I could and hoped I hadn't been seen and the horseman would quickly ride on by.

No. The hoof beats slowed from trot to walk. Then stopped. Right by me. I didn't dare look up but imagined the rider tall in his saddle just a few feet away, he must be staring in my direction. If I made myself small and stayed very still…

The horse's breath snorted into the air only an arm's length away. I could hear the shuffle of its hooves, even smell its sweat. Then I heard a voice that had once been so familiar, a voice I still heard in my dreams, a voice I had longed to hear again. It was low, not much more than a whisper.

'Amity? Is that you?'

For a moment I couldn't believe it, I pressed my hands to my side, thought I'd imagined it, that wishing had made it so.

'Amity?'

'Fin!' I whooped with laughter and rushed out to fling my arms around him. Yes! But I couldn't reach him up on his high horse. Two years is a long time.

Especially for someone just to re-appear out of the shadows with no warning.

And he looked so different. Even in the gloaming I could see he seemed much older, more serious, his shoulders broader, his hair cropped close to his skull, the curls completely gone. The Elders would be pleased about that, I thought.

Already I was asking questions. 'What are you doing on a horse? Why are you wearing that black suit and silk collar? Isn't that just for old men in The Elect? Won't you get into trouble dressed like that? Why are you here? Where have you been? What have you been doing? Where did you get the horse from?' I paused for breath.

He smiled and I felt relieved. He was still Fin, my Fin. His smile lit up his face so even in the thickening light I could see his eyes dance. Joyfully, I reached up, longing to feel his hands in mine. His smile vanished. He frowned. He looked away. His hands stayed firmly gripped on the reins of his horse so my arms waved pointlessly in mid-air and I felt foolish.

'Fin?' I said, letting arms fall hopelessly to my side. 'Fin?' I gazed up at him, trying to work out his expression, waiting for his laugh. What was Fin without his laugh? This wasn't how it was meant to be, not what I'd dreamed of for so long.

But Fin seemed to have no uncertainties. 'It's getting dark. Why are you out alone? What have you been doing?' he asked. 'And your hair…?' The briskness of his tone was as harsh as a slap. I recoiled for a moment.

But he was waiting for an answer and the angel needed help. 'A man on the beach,' I said, trying to be business-like, matter of fact. 'Not drowned but nearly.

10

I dragged him out. Left him. Was getting help.' I tried to explain, wished the man hadn't been there, that his nearly drowning was getting in the way of my reunion with Fin.

'Where?'

'Otter rocks.'

His quick look was the smallest signal of how special that place had once been to us. But the look passed as swiftly as it came. Now he was leaning down asking intently 'Has anyone else seen him? Does anyone else know he's there?'

'No. I don't think so. Only me. I was just going to get Father…'

'Well you needn't bother him.' Fin slipped his foot out of the stirrup and reached down and grabbed my arm. 'Put your foot there, that's right and now swing up! Hold on tight!'

'What?' I'd never been on a horse before.

'Hurry! We must be quick.'

Too astonished to argue, I put my foot in the stirrup and Fin hauled me up. The horse stood stock still as if he realised I didn't know what I was doing and I clambered on somehow.

'Put your arms around my waist and you won't fall off.'

I hesitated - it had been so long and he was such a stranger. But this was too good. High up, trotting along, my arms around Fin again. I clung on, leaned my head against his back, feeling the warmth of him through his jacket, his body still familiar. Without my headscarf my hair hung loose, lifted and teased by the evening air. Freedom. Fin was back. My arms were around him. This was how it was meant to be.

'When did you learn to ride?' I asked. 'Is the horse

yours? Do you look after it? How did you get it over from Mainland?'

But Fin, concentrating on the path, didn't answer. Now the horse was picking its way down to the beach and along the stream. Alongside the stepping stones the water was deep and swirled around my dangling feet but we reached the small cove safely. Fin jumped off – so elegantly as if he'd spent all his life with horses – and lifted me down. His hands were firm on my waist. I wanted to treasure the moment, make it last, but had no chance. Under the shelter of otter rocks, the angel was awake now, struggling to sit up. It was difficult, as his arm was clearly giving him pain. He said something in a language I didn't understand, English maybe. But Fin did. He answered him, carefully, in the same tongue. Another surprise. The Fin I'd known spoke only Celtic and now…

As Fin and the man talked, I felt I could almost make sense of this language, as if it were just out of reach.

Fin's face in the evening shadows was full of angles and dark hollows. He was brisk as he turned to me. This wasn't the Fin I knew, the Fin I'd thought of every day for nearly two years. 'Right I'll take care of this now,' he said. 'You must get back home as quick as you can. And Amity…"

I smiled up at him, thinking he'd take my hand, waiting for his loving words, that he'd missed me, that he'd see me the next day. But no. His voice was fierce and harsh. 'Don't tell anyone about this, Amity. No one. Or that you've seen me.'

'But..'

'Not a word! It's important. No one must know I'm here yet. Understand?'

I didn't. But because it was Fin who was asking, I nodded.

'Now go!' he said.

I turned not wanting him to see my face.

'Amity!'

I turned back, still ready again to smile.

'Your headscarf!'

He threw it at me.

Chapter 3

Shenavar

'**A**nd he didn't look at me again!' I said. 'He just bent down and started dealing with the stranger.' I looked across at Shenavar. 'I don't know if the stranger's alive or dead or who he is or where he came from. And I haven't seen or heard anything of Fin. I was sure he would have called by now but no one has even seen him… I'm beginning to think I must have dreamt the whole thing. Ohhh! What do you think Shenavar?'

Whatever Shenavar thought, I wasn't likely to find out. Shenavar was Father's grandmother and by far the oldest person on the island. She was so old that she was the only one now who could remember that other world – life before the wars more than seventy years ago. Oh that must have been wonderful with music, books, travel - planes! – freedom, all the things we didn't have any more.

Shenavar had been a heroine. It was really thanks

to her that the island survived and we're here today. But that was a very long time ago. For the last five years she'd sat slumped and silent, a tiny shell of a person who had to be fed and cared for like a baby.

Apart from a few strange noises, she never spoke. Her eyes were misty, yet sometimes, just sometimes, I saw a gleam in them that reminded me of what Shenavar was like when I was a little girl – full of stories and ideas about what life used to be like, that world full of colour and music and adventure where you could do almost anything you liked, even if you were a girl.

'Shenavar and her stories have turned your head,' my mother always used to say. 'Putting ideas in it. The world's changed. You've got to live humbly and serve the Lord and prepare yourself for being a good wife. You can forget all those stories and nonsense in books.' Mother had a particularly scornful way of saying 'books,' as if they were the work of the Devil himself.

Shenavar had shelves full of books that I'd barely had chance to look at and now never would. The Elders were scared of books. Too many ideas. Too many dreams. Too many possibilities. Unless it was the Bible, or something about diseases in chickens or how to breed pigs, they didn't want to know.

So as soon as Shenavar was taken ill, they came and took her books away and burned them. Wicked, wicked waste! Father tried to stop them but it was no good. The books were burned on the shore as a sign of how powerful the Elders thought they were.

Every year I get angrier about losing all those magical stories and the ideas that I never had the chance to explore. It just shows how weak the Elders must really be to be so frightened of words. It would have been good to write down all the stuff she told me and put it into neat little notebooks so I could look at it and keep it forever and show other people – only people I absolutely trusted, of course.

But there were hardly any pens or pencils on the island and not much paper either, certainly not enough to write down these stories. Anyway because I couldn't make a real scrapbook, I was making one in my head. Every night I concentrated hard on one little memory of things she said or stories she told so it was planted firmly in my mind like this:

Listen. *The Island never used to be an island. It was joined onto Mainland and part of the world. You could go anywhere, get in a car or a train of a plane. I flew all over, to Europe, Australia, America. The whole world was on the move for work or holidays. But of course, there were so many millions more of us then...'*

And

'If you ever get the chance again, wear bright colours, the brightest you can find. Oh and lipstick! You could wear the brightest, boldest red lipstick and look amazing.'

As if that was ever going to happen. But it was a long time now since Shenavar had told her stories and laughed at The Elders. Now people – if they thought of her at all – assumed she'd been dead for years. But I talked to her all the time, especially when I had so many words bursting inside me that I couldn't share with anyone else.

'Anyway,' I said, as I straightened her top blanket. 'I missed supper when I got back. Father made me read from the Bible while everyone else ate theirs.' I told her about how that night in the flicker of the peat fire and the glow of the wind-up hurricane lamp. I could hardly see the faces of Mother, and Father, my

16

brothers and sisters. There are ten of us altogether counting Davy. And Callum, of course. I wish Father hadn't brought Callum to live with us. Though I can't complain really because they took me in too me when I was not much more than a baby. They're the only parents I can remember.

It was nice of Lowri, the sister next to me, to smuggle up some oatcakes for me to eat in bed. 'Then she was reading her Bible' I went on to Shenavar. 'But I knew she was only reading the Song of Solomon, that bit about *the voice of my beloved*. And especially the bit about *Let him kiss me with the kisses of his mouth*. Because I think she has an eye on a lad, but I don't know which one yet.'

For a split second I could have sworn Shenavar's eyes sparkled. To be fair, I too liked that bit about kissing with the *kisses of his mouth* because it reminded me of Fin. *Kissing with the kisses of his mouth*...

I told Shenaver that I longed to tell Lowri about Fin but a promise was a promise. She'd guessed something had happened, and that I'd lied to Father when I'd said I was late because I'd been hunting for a lost knitting needle. But I couldn't tell her, so I turned over, asked God to forgive me for the lie, and pretended to go to sleep. 'Of course I didn't sleep. All I could think of was Fin, being high up on a horse with him, my arms around him, my head leaning against his back.' And the angel. 'He had the most beautiful hair and skin and eyes,' I told Shenavar, who certainly wouldn't go blabbing.

I dusted Shenavar's shelf of treasures as I talked to her, keeping my voice low so no one else in the house would hear. On the shelf was a coffee maker even though there's been no coffee on the island for seventy years or more. 'I could never start the day without two decent cups of coffee,' she used to say to me, 'And now I've survived all these years without it...' There were some pretty boxes, cups and glasses. A small gold empty tube had held lipstick, she said.

My favourite treasure of all was a snow shaker – a small globe with tiny model buildings inside and when you shook it snow swirled around and covered them. The buildings were very high, like something the little ones make out of their bricks. But Shenavar told me they were based on real buildings in a city called New York. In those days there were so many people that they had to live on top of each other right up into the sky. New York isn't there any more. It was destroyed early in the wars and all its millions of people with it.

When I was little I used to love the snow shaker but now when I picked it up I thought of all those buildings toppling and the people gone, and all the millions more in the thousands of cities all over the world... I shivered and went back to a much more interesting topic. 'Why do you think Fin is back?' I asked Shenavar. 'And why is he dressed like the Elect? And why couldn't I tell anyone he was home?'

'It must be a Fin joke,' I answered myself. 'Maybe he'd "borrowed" the smart suit and the horse just for a laugh, to see if he could. That's it. Of course. That would be such a Fin trick.' But, I thought gloomily, that didn't explain how he could ride so well. Or speak English. Or seemed ... so different.

'He'll turn up, won't he?' I said 'Soon?'

There was a knock on the door, a kerfuffle in the kitchen. 'It must be him!' I said gleefully, dropping the snow shaker in an instant. 'He's come to see me!'

Chapter 4

Visitors

I dashed to the door, jumping over baby Liam who was sitting in the middle of the kitchen floor banging a pan with a wooden spoon.

Mother was working at the kitchen table on a television set. They still got washed ashore sometimes. I knew what they used to be for, of course. Shenavar had told me all about them. But now they were treasured because if you could get the screen off the front it was useful for glass. We had no way of making glass and with all the storms we had lots of broken windows. Mother had the right mix of delicate skill and strength to get the screens off unbroken. This was a big one which would nearly fill a window.

'Come in!' she called, as she gently levered up a corner of the screen and eased the sides out. But whoever was outside wasn't wandering in like our neighbours normally do but was waiting politely outside.

'Come yourself in!' called my mother again. 'Why people can't just get on and not expect to be waited on...' She concentrated on the screen which came out with a satisfying *ping*.

I skidded to the door, took a deep breath and flung it open with a huge smile, my heart thudding, to welcome Fin. Only it wasn't. It was Idris Mordecai. Idris Mordecai is a sheep. Not a real one, you understand, but not very far removed. He's the same age as me and left school at the same time as the girls because, frankly, he's pretty dim. His face is long and blank as a sheep and he has a way of standing with his head tilted to one side. You almost expect him to say 'Baaaaa..'

'Oh hello Amity" he said, looking down at his feet. 'Is, I was wondering, that is. Perhaps...'

'If you want Father, he's probably in the barn' I said, peering beyond him down the road in case Fin was coming.

'Well no,' said Idris staring at me, 'Not really. 'He looked at his feet again. 'Well, that is yes, right, yes.'

There was a wail. Baby Liam had banged himself on the head with the wooden spoon. 'Sorry Idris. Got to go. Try the barn for Father.' And I shut the door on him firmly.

When you're expecting someone like Fin, finding Idris Mordecai on the doorstep is a deep disappointment.

I was chopping onions for the soup - onions! My hands would stink! - when the next knock came. I plunged my hands into cold water thinking it would take the smell away and was just drying them on my apron when the door opened.

Fin! No. My heart sank.

'Good day, sirs,' said my mother curtseying to the visitors. Three old men in dark suits and solemn faces strode in, filling the room with their musty blackness. These were the Elders who came once a month to bring Shenavar her medicine. Not just stuff from Dr John, this was special stuff brought over from the Mainland, so we were supposed to be grateful.

They looked carefully at Shenavar, slumped in her chair. 'We shall pray for our sister in her suffering,' they said in chorus and then bowed their heads, each one taking it in turn to recite a prayer. Though I stood with my head bowed, I hated them for not being Fin and willed them to go. Each time I thought they'd finished, I'd look up in relief, then they'd they start on another prayer and I'd have to stand with head bowed again, listening desperately in case Fin came to the door. When they finally left, Shenavar seemed nearly as restless as me. 'Here,' I said. 'Have your phone.'

Now this is the oddest of her treasures. Just a small rectangle of metal with plastic on the front. Many times Shenavar had tried to tell me what her phone could do but when she talked about instant communication and instant access to all the world's knowledge and music all in that one little bit of metal and plastic, she lost me. That really was the weirdest of her fairy stories.

Still, Shenavar liked her phone. I put it in her hand and watched her fingers curl around it and, as always, she tapped the front of it with her thumb. Like baby Liam and his blanket, it gave her some comfort. As she stroked her phone, I day-dreamed of Fin. Please let him come soon! But the angel stranger kept drifting into my thoughts too, with his golden skin and golden hair.

We had three more visitors that afternoon, none of them Fin. By the time the little ones came home from school and Father and Callum came in from work I was as jumpy as a cat. Father didn't take his jacket off when he came in. Instead he said 'Amity will you come here a moment, child.' And he led me out of the house again, down the path towards the barn, Nutmeg our sheepdog following at his heels.

'Father?' I wondered what was going on.

He walked down to the old bench where Mother sometimes sat to feed the baby on one of our rare sunny days. On the wall behind us, a thick old stem of ivy, dead we thought for years, had put out tiny tendrils, so green and bright. I noticed the clean smell of earth as if things were growing. Father sat down and patted the bench. I sat beside him. 'I had a visitor this afternoon,' he said.

My heart lurched. Had Fin come to see Father already? 'Who?' I asked. I could hardly breathe waiting to hear what Father would say and bent down to hide my face and tickle Nutmeg's ears.

'Idris Mordecai.'

Arrgghh! My head shot back up again in horror. That's twice in one day Idris Mordecai had invaded my world.

'Oh,' I said. What had this to do with me? Why was Father bothering to tell me? Nutmeg, cross because I'd stopped tickling his ears, nuzzled his head into my hand.

Father's big and solid and not given much to laughter. But he's not cruel. He never whipped me. I didn't have to curtsey to him as some of the girls had to with their fathers, or stand with my eyes down. I could look him directly in the eye. Sometimes, despite his sternness he smiled back. Today his expression was inscrutable. I had no idea what he was going to say. He looked at me carefully. 'Idris Mordecai has asked for your hand in marriage.'

Something happened to my brain. I heard Father's words. I knew what they meant but they made no sense to me. I must have sat gawping for a long time because finally Father said gently 'Child…?'

Then his words came crashing into my head, like thundering waves in a big black storm and I knew exactly what they meant and I leapt up from the bench.

'Idris?!' I said 'Marry?! Me marry Idris Mordecai? Why? Where has this came from? What made him think…?'

'He's a good reliable lad,' said my father. 'A hard worker.'

'But he's a sheep!' I squawked and the corners of Father's mouth twitched.

'He's certainly very good with sheep,' he said carefully.

'But not with people!' I said. 'Idris Mordecai! Never! '

'And have you done anything to encourage his hopes? Has he not spoken to you, given you even a hint of how he felt?'

'No! Father – it's Idris! I never even speak to him unless I really, really have to. Well, there was that time I helped rescue one of his sheep that was trapped in the gorse bush on the cliff. But that was on account of the poor sheep, not Idris.'

Father nodded and gave me a sharp look. 'And he wasn't the reason you spent so long looking for your knitting needle last night?'

'No,' I said. My cheeks burned. 'No. It was nothing to do with anything like that.' I didn't like lying to Father, but I'd made a promise to Fin.

'Most of your schoolfellows have been married this long time and are already mothers. Your mother is getting anxious for you. You are of an age...'

'I understand Father,' I said trying to keep the panic out of my voice. 'But not just yet, please, *please*.'

I longed to tell him that in a few days I might be telling him I'd be marrying Fin but still sworn to secrecy I kept my tongue curbed except to say 'Please Father, please not Idris!'

'Right,' said my father, getting up from the bench. 'I shall tell the young man he is to be disappointed and he is better looking elsewhere. To be true, I would not say you were a pair best suited.'

Nutmeg licked my hand. Maybe he was pleased too. We went back into the house.

'Be kind to your mother child,' he said before he opened the door. 'She wants only the best for your future.'

As we went in Mother looked up and could see instantly what my answer had been. 'You stupid, stupid girl!' she snapped, banging a dish down on to the table so hard that it set baby Liam off wailing. 'What makes you think anyone else will come asking for you? 'It is your duty, child, your *duty* to marry! Can't you see that?'

'I...' I caught Father's eye, so I bit my tongue and lowered my eyes and let Mother shout.

I ate my supper meekly and did all my chores before Mother could ask me. Oh please Fin, I prayed silently to myself. Please don't wait any longer.

Listen. *'I wish I could tell you how much colour there was in the world…a spring day with a clear blue sky, green leaves and bright yellow daffodils or red tulips, bright and dazzling. Our homes were full of colour. As for our clothes… But it was that dazzling green of spring after a long winter that made our spirits soar. One day, when the clouds have burnt themselves out and the air is clean again, really clean, I hope you'll know that feeling.'*

Chapter 5

Waiting

'Idris Mordecai! Baa baa baa!' Lowri was laughing so much she was nearly crying. Bekah laughed too and even Susannah, nursing her new baby, smiled over the top of her infant's head.

I spluttered, 'What gave him the idea? I've hardly even talked to him apart from being polite and rescuing his silly sheep!' I said.

'You must have smiled at him in that certain way…' said Bekah.

'Or just been kind to him,' said Susannah. 'I don't think many people are kind to poor Idris.'

'What a wonderful marriage you would have,' said Lowri. 'You could talk about sheep. And sheep. And maybe sometimes, sheep…'

'But at least,' said Susannah, suddenly serious, 'Idris would be kind. And I think that's an important thing in a husband.'

'Baa' giggled Lowri.

Susannah's other two little boys playing on the rug in front of the fire looked surprised and joined in making baahing noises. I laughed too – if only to stop myself thinking about when Fin would turn up and what had happened about the angel.

Mother clearly hadn't forgiven me for rejecting Idris's offer. She must have thought Lowri and I needed a good example of happy marriage so she'd sent us over to see Susannah, with pans of soup and puddings. Susannah had just had a baby, her third in two years. And she was still only seventeen...

'Be fruitful and increase in numbers.' We had a whole world to populate, the Elders told us, keen to marry us off as soon as possible. Susannah and Euan seemed happy enough but I never knew how much choice Susannah had about marrying him.

Bekah had come with me. She was quite ridiculous about babies and was already reaching out to take the baby from Susannah.

'Haven't you got the chubbiest wubbiest little pink cheeks?' she drooled over him. 'He's beautiful!' she said to Susannah, who beamed proudly. 'Isn't he beautiful, Amity?'

'Of course he is,' I said, though to be honest he looked just like every other new baby, pink and creased and cross. The two little boys, carried away by their baaing and giggles, now started hitting each other. The little one howled and Susannah eased herself carefully out of her chair.

'It's alright, I'll get them something to eat,' I said and set some of the soup to warm by the fire while sorting out spoons and bowls for the boys.

Lowri handed over a small bottle of one of her home-made potions. 'For the soreness,' she said to

Susannah. I didn't want to think about the soreness. But Lowri's very good at making lotions and potions. Dr John thinks she's has great healing skills.

'Grandfather said to tell you he's found a new willow tree growing by the stream on the other side of the hill,' said Bekah. 'It's still very small but looks healthy so should grow. He said the infusion you made for him when he was ill in the winter really helped.'

Lowri was pleased. 'The bark is so good for pain and fever. If we can get more willows to grow it could make a real difference.'

Their talk rambled around plants and pain and I don't know what. I wasn't really listening as I kept glancing out of the tiny window - most of it was boarded up for lack of glass - wondering if I might see Fin out there. I didn't know if I was looking for the old Fin who'd filled my memory for nearly two years with his laughing face and curly hair, or the new sombre Fin in black coat and cropped skull…

I lifted the small boys up to the scrubbed wooden table and dished out some soup. I had to sit with baby Jamie and carefully spoon it in while he wailed snotty tears because he wanted his mother to do it. Soup and snot and tears and dribble ran down his chin together. It didn't make me want to have babies.

'Have you heard from Davy or Fin?' asked Bekah.

What? Did Bekah know something? But her round face was as pretty and as straightforward as ever. I wished I could tell her about my meeting with Fin.

'Maybe he'll be back soon,' said Bekah happily. 'And then it will be you and him with a houseful of babies.'

Lowri snorted with laughter. 'Bekah! Don't start Amity off again!'

I couldn't help it. 'When Fin comes back, we'll

both leave this island,' I said, slowly, trying not to get angry, 'and go far away and find different places and different ways of doing things.'

'But you don't know what you'd find!' said Bekah, horrified. 'It would be terrible and dangerous.'

'Of course it could. But maybe it isn't. Anyway, I want to know.'

'Why?' Bekah always asked. 'Why would you want to leave what we've got here? The fires of Hell are still burning there. Nearly everyone in Outland was killed in the wars or died of the smoke or starvation or disease. How do those left manage to live? And the rats, Amity, think of the rats! They say that Outland is over-run with rats the size of dogs!'

Suzannah and Lowri shivered at the thought. 'And what about the White Star states?' asked Susannah,' Euan says there could be more war.'

'When Davy and Fin come home we'll have everything we want here.' Bekah went on. 'And our own babies...'

She kissed the new baby's toes again. All Bekah has ever wanted is to be settled down with Davy and a house full of children.

'Everything? *Everything?* Is this all you want?' I shot back smartly 'Always doing what you're told, not allowed to think for yourself. Do you never, *ever,* want to get off this island and see more of the world?'

Bekah looked puzzled and a bit hurt and asked 'What exactly is it you want, Amity?'

'Oh I don't *know!* That was the really frustrating thing. I didn't know exactly. 'Just more than this. There must be more than this. If I'd been a boy I might have been an Engineer and at least I'd have got as far as the rigs or Mainland!'

We were stranded on the island. The waters between us and Mainland were deep and dangerous. So many young men had died in its torrents that the Elders had forbidden any more to try. It was a rare day, perhaps once in a few weeks that even the Engineers' boat could make a crossing. In winter it could easily be months.

The Alliance still had great skills in making power from the wind. But we had no metal-making - and little to make metal from - and great plans would be delayed for want of something simple as nails or the right tools.

'Can't you feel something in the air?' I pleaded with them. 'Can't you feel, oh, that something's about to happen? That everything's going to change?'

They looked at me blankly. I was desperate for the others to see the world as I did but they never did.

'Hush now' laughed Susannah, easing her soft, milky body into a more comfortable position. 'You two will never agree so I don't know why you keep on arguing. Some of us have to have babies or what will happen to us all?'

'The trouble with you, Amity,' she said, 'is that you've spent too long with Shenavar. The old lady always had strange ideas, didn't she? All that travelling, all those books, all that learning. Did she really tell the Elders off?'

'Oh yes,' I said. 'I was only little but I'll never forget. They came in, all in their black suits and their serious faces, looking for sin. She told them she remembered them as priggish little schoolboys and if their God was as grim and joyless as they were then she wanted nothing to do with Him. Or them. They could hardly believe what she was saying. Oh their faces!' I laughed at the memory.

'But then next day she had the stroke.' No laughing matter at all.

'The Elders tried to make it was because she was blasphemous. But she was very old. It could have happened at any time, no matter what they said in church.'

I spooned the last of the soup into a wailing Jamie and was just washing the boys' hands and faces when we heard a noise outside. A gang of small boys, my brothers Iolo and Bryn among them, were hurtling through the village shouting.

'The traders are coming! The traders are coming!'

They whooped and called and ran on shouting.

The traders! Lowri, Bekah and I said a hasty goodbye to Susannah and ran.

Listen. *'That first bleak black winter we went scavenging in the shops and houses that were left. Once we found a box of brightly patterned bikinis. Not much use. Until we realised it must be Christmas so we hung them up above the fireplace like decorations. They looked good and made us smile, which was the important bit.'*

Chapter 6

The Traders

We were in such a hurry that we didn't even bother to knit as we raced along.

As we got close to home I could see the first of the heavy horse-drawn wagons coming plod, plod, plod down the rutted roadway. Indoors, Mother was all of a panic.

'Amity, Lowri! Quick now. There's so much to take!' She was already at the big cupboard sorting out the work we'd knitted over the winter, ready for this day. Thick jumpers with elaborate patterns, warm soft socks, heavy jackets, caps, shawls, scarves the little ones had made, were all stored in carefully hoarded carrier bags washed up on the shore.

'Right, Elspeth, Morag, have you washed your hands? Right then, take these please! Hold them carefully, don't run. Take them over to the hall. And here's a blanket your father made. Too good for us to use. That must go to the traders.'

The traders had told us long ago that there were people who valued our knitting and were prepared to pay for it. I didn't know who these people were but the island's knitted clothes, the lacy shawls, intricate jackets, fine cardigans were highly prized on Mainland so we sent our best work to them. Who were these people who could wear fancy clothes and pay for them? What was their world like? Different from ours, that's for sure. Apart from one piece for Sundays and special occasions perhaps, the island women themselves never wore their own work. It was much too good for our everyday lives.

'Couldn't we keep one of the jumpers?' asked Elspeth. 'The blue one I knitted is so pretty…'

'No child!' snapped Mother. 'You must offer your work up to God and remember humility.'

Elspeth made a face and I tried to imagine what it was like to wear something pretty just for the sake of pretty.

'Vanity, vanity, all is vanity,' said Mother, as so often breaking into my thoughts.

'Right come on, all of you. Amity, Lowri, Elspeth, Charity, Morag, step sharply.' Mother led the way and we followed in a little procession, all of us balancing great parcels in our arms.

We weren't the only ones.

The whole island seemed to be gathering at the hall, women and children all carefully carrying precious garments, which they placed on tables already covered with white cloths, patched and darned but spotlessly clean. Mothers fussed, making sure everything was displayed to its best advantage. Even Mrs Chief Elder and the other elders' wives were there, their knitting on a table apart, though it was no better than ours.

As well as the jackets and shawls I'd added to Mother's store, I had something else that she didn't know about, something that I knew she wouldn't approve of and so I'd knitted and kept in Shenavar's room...

'Oh I love it when the traders come,' I said to Lowri as we marched briskly along behind Mother.

'So do I! A chance for something new and some treats,' she said, struggling to keep hold of her heap of carefully wrapped knitting.

'It's not just that. It's because they go everywhere, been everywhere. They're proof that there really is a world beyond the island. That it's not just us.'

The wagons parked up outside the community hall. First of all were the heavy carts laden with official supplies. You could never guarantee what the traders could find and bring but with luck there would be spare parts for the turbines, corrugated iron for shelters, ropes, nails, screws, tools, shotgun cartridges, plumbing pipes and joints, ingots of iron for Tom Watts the blacksmith, medicines for Dr John. Each wagon was drawn by a team of four or six huge horses.

The men got busy unloading and putting stuff in store. After the storms of winter there was plenty to repair and they'd been waiting anxiously for the traders with the supplies.

The really interesting stuff came after the heavy wagons - smaller carts, piled high with bolts of material, sacks of flour, and sugar, tubs of salt and who knows what other riches. The traders jumped down, stretching themselves after the journey, while their children scampered here and there glad to be able to run free after miles in the wagons.

The village air was suddenly alive with noise, shrill voices, whistles and cheery shouts as the traders set up.

The traders were a race apart. They were small, dark, sharp-featured and sharp-eyed, they spoke our own Celtic well enough but with a strong accent. No one knew where they came from. They arrived unannounced once or twice a year, when the waters were calm and the Engineers could ferry them across to the makeshift jetty on the far side of the island. They traded all over Mainland, the South and even Outland and always had the smell of oily smoke and mystery about them. These days they were the only ones who roamed the across countries.

'They're scavengers,' Father would say. 'But we couldn't have survived much longer without them. They go through the choking smoke into the ruins of towns and cities where no one else will go for fear of rats and plague and see what they can find. They make big profits but they risk their lives and health to get hold of their goods. They do a useful service and grow rich on it. But until we can make things for ourselves again we're beholden to them.'

Before she was ill Shenevar, of course, would always go and talk to them, sit on the steps of their wagons and chat openly to the traders and their wives. Nobody else ever did that. They certainly didn't now.

Traders didn't just bring us essential supplies – wherever they got them from – but they also brought us news. From them we knew how the great hell fires were burning in the once oil-rich lands. We knew things were changing when the black clouds didn't come so often but we didn't know what was happening in the lands bordering Mainland and had no idea about anywhere else. Only the traders could tell us more. This was what I craved, a link to the rest of the world.

But they wouldn't be rushed. First of all they uncoupled their horses and let them loose on the patch behind the hall where grass grew quite strongly. Then they talked to the men. I scooted over to hang around at the edge of the group, hoping to hear what was going on, to hear some scrap of news of the world beyond the island.

While a few of the traders checked lists with the Elders, the rest rocked on their heels, drank mugs of milk brought to them by the women. They looked around them. One of them - I heard them call him Xander - looked at me quite openly and winked. I blushed and looked away quickly. Then finally, as if underlining that this was all in their own time, they came into the hall and looked at what we had.

All the island women had arranged their knitting on tables and stood anxiously by as the traders looked at their handiwork, handled some of the stuff, picked some and then handed over metal tokens from a big leather bag. Xander strode past the table where all the elders' wives waited grandly behind their knitting and came straight away to where Mother and we all were waiting.

'Ah mistress, I know I can always trust yours to be the best quality,' he said, polite as you like when talking to Mother. He certainly wasn't going to wink at her. Behind him was a young boy. The trader nodded at all the socks and the young lad took them and scampered off. He was back in seconds to collect Father's fine blanket.

'No tweed this year?' asked Xander.

'No, sir, we've needed it for jackets and trousers for our own men-folk. So many young men shooting up now and no clothes to put on their backs,' said Mother.

'Yes, you've a growing population, right enough. It's as well that everything else is growing to keep them fed. You're a lot luckier than many.'

I could see Mother was longing to give him the talk about being God's Chosen Ones but she managed not to as the trader looked through every single jumper and jacket that Mother and Lowri and Ellen and Elspeth and Morag and I had knitted and bought the lot. He studied each one, fingered it and nodded. The young lad would take them, dart off and come back. Then 'What's this?' he asked. And he looked straight at me as though he knew I was the one who'd made it. It was the shawl I'd knitted in secret in Shenavar's room. I'd deliberately put it on the table under one of Mother's jumpers.

'I've never seen that!' snapped my mother.

'So did you make this?' asked the trader, ignoring her furious stare and looking at me. His eyes were deep, dark brown and diamond sharp.

I nodded. It was a shawl but not one to clutch round on a winter's day just to keep you warm. This was a shawl I imagined from Shenavar's stories, a shawl for queen or a princess, a shawl to frame a face and make her look more beautiful. It was as light as a feather, a wisp of a shawl, a dream of a shawl. I'd spun the wool extra fine, dyed it with bilberry juice so that the colours ranged from palest pink to deepest purple and I'd knitted it on needles so slender that I was scared of snapping them.

It was all very fanciful really and I'm not sure why

37

I'd put so much effort into it. I'd worked on it in Shenavar's room while I talked to her, afraid that Mother would dismiss it as too frivolous. But I'd been so tired of making things that were just so *useful*. Was it so wrong to make something that was just beautiful? Mother would probably think so. That's why I'd hidden it in a bag in Shenavar's cupboard, the bag that had strange writing on the side. *Riverside Designer Outlet*. Shenavar had once tried to explain that to me but I couldn't make any sense of it.

Now Mother was frowning. 'What a waste of wool and time!' she snapped.

But the trader handled the shawl, running it gently through his rough fingers as though he appreciated its fineness. He smiled and nodded to himself and then handed me the tokens. With a quick sideways glance at Mother, he counted them out slowly into my hand. There were more tokens than I expected, more even than for an intricately patterned jumper.

'Eight, nine, ten…' the more he counted them out into my hand, the lower Mother's jaw dropped in astonishment. 'You could make some more of these for next time I come,' he said and looked at Mother, so surprised she was dumbstruck - which doesn't happen often.

'Oh yes, ma'am. The world is waking up again and there'll always be people who have a yearning for some luxury. Even now. Especially now.'

'The world is waking up? How?' I asked. 'What's happening there in the world?' I wanted to know everything he could tell me.

But the trader just gave a slow glance at my mother and back at me and said nothing. Just smiled and walked away, carrying the shawl himself instead of trusting it to his boy. I handed the tokens straight over to my mother. I knew she wanted to talk sharply to me, but the sight and weight of the tokens in her hand stopped her words before they could take breath. 'Let's go and see what there is to buy,' she finally said.

I looked over my shoulder at the trader and longed to talk to Xander. Out there was a world where people loved and wanted beautiful things just for the sake of their beauty. And he could tell me all about it. How different from the island it must be, I thought. How very different...

Ouch! My mother tugged my arm. 'Come along girl, stop dreaming! We have things to buy!' We made our way down the wagons.

'Have you any waterproofs?' Mother asked the first trader. Waterproofs were prized above rubies. The few we had were worn and torn to shreds, stuck together with tape, which was also hard to get. Keeping dry on the island was a constant challenge. Getting up and putting on clothes still damp from the day before was misery.

But the trader shook his head. 'Sorry, lady. Not this time...'

Mother sighed. 'Perhaps next time,' she said. 'Right let's look at material.'

Everything we had had been patched and darned and the worn bits cut away until in the end one of Father's old shirts worked its way all through the family until there was barely enough left for a vest for the baby.

Traders had long bundles of cloth on display. Mother chose quickly, mainly dull and sober colours. But I spotted a roll in bright yellow. 'Oh Lowri, look!'

I cried as I reached out to it. 'It's the colour of sunshine. Doesn't it make your heart sing just to look at it? It would have made some bonny blouses or a dress.' Mother just raised her eyes to Heaven as if the Devil himself was tempting her, pushed it to one side and chose something grey. The trader grinned sympathetically.

Then there were needles and thread and buttons to buy, a new pair of scissors, a kettle, some pans, a sharp knife to replace the one Jamie had lost and some spoons because ours had just vanished. There was wheat flour and yeast so we could have bread as well as oatcakes, a barrel of salt to preserve the mutton and bacon and fish; a bag of sugar, vinegar for pickling. Sometimes the store had these things, sometimes they didn't. 'It's always best to have your own,' said Mother.

The tokens were nearly running out now. Mother managed to find some new rubber boots for Father, 'a bit big, but he can wear two pairs of socks' and then went and had a final stroll past the parade of wagons.

I wanted to know where all these things had come from. Tried to imagine the deserted warehouses in a ruined landscape, abandoned towns and factories. The traders ventured far from the Mainland of the Celtic Alliance right into the lost and dark lands where the pall of smoke had never yet broken up. That really must be like the jaws of Hell.

All the time we walked among the stalls I kept my eyes open for a tall young member of the Elect.

Mother knew exactly which traders she would buy from. From one she bought a packet of tea, 'Ah, all winter I've been dreaming of a good cup of tea,' she said.

'We don't know if we'll be able to get any more,' said the trader. 'Stocks are low and we've not heard of any plantations growing again. No news is getting through. No news means no boats, means no tea. This might be the last chance...'

Mother quickly took another packet. 'And one more.' From another stall she bought a small packet of tobacco for Father, who had spent the last four months sucking on an empty pipe. Then she spied some dried fruit. She sniffed it carefully 'Hmmm, hardly any smell of smoke and oil,' she said 'Right! We shall have tea and cake tonight.'

'Hooray! shouted Iolo as Mother pressed more packages onto us all so we all looked just like the traders' packhorses.

Finally, she handed over the last of the tokens to a trader, who filled a paper bag full of brightly coloured sweets as the little ones cheered. Mother smiled. It was a rare sight, like winter sunshine and so even more precious.

That evening my mother carefully transferred the tea into the battered old tea caddy that commemorated King William and Queen Catherine's coronation. It was a long time since it had been full of tea. Then she made welshcakes, small flat cakes with raisins, over the kitchen fire. Such a treat. We ate them warm off the griddle and washed them down with tea. I took one of them through to Shenavar, carefully breaking it up so she could manage it without choking.

Our house was full of warmth and the rich smell of fruit and sugar and a feeling of contentment. 'Isn't this wonderful?' sighed Lowri as she took a second cup of tea, holding the mug between her hands and breathing in the scent of it before she even sipped it.

'It is,' I said. 'So it is.'

'Then why do you look so worried?' laughed Lowri. 'This is the best day of the year and you're as jumpy as a cat.'

I couldn't tell her about Fin. Or the angel. I just wish I knew where they were, what was going on. Anxiety about them nibbled at my insides in the same way as I nibbled the welshcakes. I longed for Father to come home, to see if he had any news.

Father and Callum had been with the men in the community hall, taking a dram with the traders - the only time island men ever had a drink. It was the first time Callum had joined them and the first time he'd ever tasted whisky. When they finally arrived home, he could hardly walk straight and looked even more foolish than usual.

'Well, what news from the world?' asked Mother, pretending not to notice Callum's struggle to find a stool to sit on. Not even she wanted to spoil the happy mood in the house. Callum's legs wouldn't obey him and we could see he was astonished by this. Lowri and Elspeth were trying not to giggle.

'There are stirrings in Outland,' said Father, ignoring Callum. 'They have news – I know not how – that some of the fires have burned themselves out though it is clear that no one will be able to live in those places for years, if ever again. The soil is so blighted, the seas and rivers are dead. From the middle of Europe south there is still black smoke and little sign of life.'

'But in the north they say there is movement. More groups of people have found each other and small towns have grown up. There is more trading, more organisation. The air is clear and they've cleared more ground and are beginning to settle now they can grow a few crops and not exist just by scavenging. They're even beginning to make things. There are people making iron again, actually making it, not just scavenging old stocks. The world is really moving on. But the people need power, especially oil. And we have plenty of that.'

Mother relaxing over her tea, looked shocked. 'But that's ours! They can't have it! They don't deserve it! We are the chosen people. We live by God's rules and that's why He saved us and our power. We can't go giving them away!'

'Why not?' asked Father, carefully packing some of the new tobacco into his pipe. He took a taper to the fire, lit his pipe and sucked happily. 'Doesn't the Bible tell us to love our neighbour as ourselves? In any case, it would be to the benefit of us all. There are people out there who have skills and knowledge that we lack and need. We cannot live forever with what the traders can scavenge. There are too few of us to do much more. If we want to build our New Jerusalem, a new world for us all, then we need to join together.'

'But the Elders!' said Mother looking frightened.

'The Elders,' said Father firmly, drawing on his pipe, 'are not always right. They are so full of their own importance as God's representatives on earth that they have forgotten the real purpose of why we are here and what we must do.'

'Husband!' gasped Mother, shocked, She looked around as if scared that the Elders might hear, as if they might be perching on the mantelpiece –which, knowing them, wouldn't actually surprise me - but she didn't say anything more. It wasn't a wife's place to argue with her husband.

'There is more,' said Father. 'There's a new threat, not just from the fringes of Mainland and Outland but from over the snowy wastes, the White Star states. They have some oil of their own but not enough. They want ours and they will not ask but just take it if they get the chance.' I wanted Father to say more but he didn't want to upset Mother any more so he just took a welshcake and said 'Aahh! Now that's a real treat.'

Mother smiled nervously. Then she asked. 'Was there no news from Davy?'

'Not this time,' said Father. 'He can't always be there at the right time for the traders. Have no fear. If there were anything amiss we'd have heard. No news is good news.'

Really? It didn't seem like that to me. I did try to enjoy my tea but all I could think of was when I would see Fin, what had happened to the angel. But all these threats hung in the air, spoiling everything like the black oily clouds.

Callum sat up blearily. Drink did him no good. He looked so silly that I started to laugh. 'The tradersh said there was a shpy,' he said, his voice loud, his words slurred. 'A spy washed ashore.'

'Oh,' I said, and the laugh died instantly. My heart thudded as I tried not to appear too interested in his words. 'What happened to him?'

'Prayed over him,' said Callum, then slumped back down on the stool. 'Then they must have shot him. Good thing too.' And he slid from the stool in a heap.

Listen. *Before the wars started you could buy nearly everything you wanted – as long as you had money. Even if you didn't, you could get easy credit. Even the poorest in our country never starved. There were shops everywhere – massive shops, a hundred times the size of our church here, rows and rows of them, full of endless shelves full of everything you ever wanted and things you didn't know you wanted until you saw them...*

It was a shock to have nothing. We had to learn quickly or die.'

Chapter 7

Xander

I stood for a moment outside Susannah's little house, straightened my skirt, smoothed my hair, checked my headscarf and then walked very slowly down the main street. Quickly I glanced to right and left in case Fin could be seen but there was no sign of him.

'Are you looking for someone, Amity?' The voice at my shoulder was sickly sweet. It belonged to Priscilla, grand-daughter of Mr and Mrs Chief Elder. Priscilla is two years younger than I am, very neat and very pretty and very pious. Everyone thinks she's wonderful. Unless they know her…

'No, Priscilla. I'm just having a moment's thankfulness for such a glorious day,' I said, with a perfectly straight face. That should keep her quiet.

No such luck. She walked beside me, smiling - modestly and humbly of course - at everyone going past. 'It was just that you seemed a little anxious Amity,' she said in her oh-so-concerned tones.

'Not at all,' I said, as airily as I could manage. 'Should I be?'

'Oh no, I'm sure not,' she said. 'But if you are, you know, you can always come and talk to me.' And she turned off into her grandparents' house.

I tried to imagine a world in which I was so desperate for conversation that I would willingly have talked to Priscilla. I couldn't. But she was right. I was certainly anxious. Anyway, what did she know?

I almost asked her about the angel. Was he the spy that Callum had talked about? Would they really have shot him? And what about Fin? Maybe they'd shot him too and that was why he hadn't been to see me. I felt sick, as though someone had taken out my heart and squeezed it out tight like a dishcloth.

Despite the comfort of proper tea and warm welshcakes, I'd lain awake most of last night trying to make sense of Callum's drunken ramblings. I'd asked Father outright about the spy but he'd said he knew nothing. He'd been with a different group of men from Callum and certainly hadn't heard anything. But a spy, washed ashore – it was too near what had happened not to have some truth in it.

So on my way to work in the polytunnels this morning, I called in on Susannah and hoped that her Euan might have heard something and told her when he got home.

'No,' she laughed. 'He can't take the whisky and wouldn't remember anything. He burbled about the White Star states and the threat but what I mainly heard was there was nothing as good as a proper drink with friends and neighbours. Over and over again. He has a dreadful head on him this morning and serve him right.'

I held her baby and changed his nappy (*yuk!*) while she sorted out Jamie and Lachlan. Then I said, 'I'd better get to work.' And I dashed off, wondering where to get news. Meeting Priscilla had made it worse. After all, she might have heard something through her grandparents. But I couldn't ask her.

I walked past Bekah's house with its pots and tubs of flowers. She was the only one to bother with flowers. Most islanders gave up on flowers in the smoke and wind and oily, salty air. But Bekah, her mother and grandfather had the knack of growing things in big pots, sheltered between makeshift fences. Behind the house, next to the weaving shed, they had a small lean-to building which still had some glass. Here things could grow, warm and sheltered from the wind and black clouds. Not having lots of babies gave them time for other things. Their house was always a splash of colour in the grey landscape. I don't think the Elders approved of that either. *Much too frivolous.*

Otherwise it was just the usual morning sights. Women carrying big baskets of washing going back and forth to the communal laundry, or carrying items from the store, or going to work in the big polytunnels, or bringing in peat from the stacks beside each house. They mostly had children clinging to their skirts or playing at their heels or falling over or crying for attention.

Other children were climbing in and out of cars. Nearly every house had a car. Some families used it as an extra storage space, handy to keep fuel dry near the back door, or to store sacks of feed, or skinned rabbits. Others let children use the cars as climbing frames. The tyres had long gone to make swings for the children to play on, or for use as bumper protectors in the days when we still had boats, or even shoes. Seats had been taken out and moved into houses so growing families could sit down. And the windows, of course. Many a broken window was replaced with a car windscreen.

I passed the ruins of a big van. The wheels had gone, the glass had gone and I knew its back doors were part of a fence at the top of the island. But if you looked very carefully you could see it once had *Global logistics. Next day UK delivery* painted on its side. But now the letters were faded, the van had no wheels and was used as a hen house. Shenavar had told me what the label meant. Imagine being able to get to anywhere in the UK the *very next day*…

Now I got my needles out. Even as we walked between house and work, if we had hands free, we all knitted. We all did this from the time we were about five years old. Constantly. Our knitting sheaths hung from our belts and never a moment was wasted, because as The Elders kept telling us, the Devil makes work for idle hands. So our hands were never ever allowed to be idle. Though, believe me, there was never much chance to be idle on the island.

I was working on a jacket for Bryn. If you took the untreated wool and knitted it very tight, it was nearly as waterproof as when it was on the sheep and it served well enough for the cold wet days of winter. I would never take fine work out of the house, especially this new shawl I was planning. I bent my head and fussed with the needles for a moment, pretending there was a knot in the wool, anything to give me a few extra moments out in the street, a few extra moments when Fin might come by.

The last of the traders' wagons was pulling off now. I loved the sound they made, the creak and sway. It was as if it reminded me of something, but I didn't know what. Perhaps it was like the creaks on a big boat, sailing over the sea...

The trader, Xander, who'd winked at me the night before and bought my fine shawl, was now tying down a tarpaulin cover stretched over the load, tugging it sharply to get it as tight as possible. 'Good morning, miss,' he said to me, politely enough yet with a sort of knowing grin in his manner.

'Good morning,' I returned barely lifting my eyes.

'It's a fine day, miss,' he said. 'And how's the old lady? I didn't get a chance last night to see her or to ask your Da.'

'The old lady?' I was so startled I looked up and straight at him. 'You mean Shenavar?'

'Aye, a grand old woman. More courage than a dozen men. She was a great friend of my old grandfather. He often spoke of her and their adventures together.'

Adventures together? What was all that? I don't remember those stories...

'But Grandfather died during this last winter. The smoke got him in the end and I wondered about the old lady.' He shouldn't really be speaking to me. I shouldn't really be replying. But he was polite enough. I remembered Shenavar sitting on the wagon steps chatting to the traders.

Of course, it couldn't really be sinful to be doing this. I straightened my shoulders. 'She lives still,' I said. 'But it is no life. She doesn't speak, hardly moves. Just gets sort of smaller as though she's shrinking away.'

'Ah, yes. That's the way of it missy, and I'm sorry for the news. But what a life she had! What a life. But of course, you'd know that more than most.'

No I didn't! What did he mean? I wanted to ask him what he knew of Shenavar and how she knew his grandfather and everything. But there was something even more important I had to know and this was my only chance. 'Excuse me. But would you know anything about a spy?' I asked looking into his weatherbeaten face and his dark eyes.

'A spy?' He was smiling, his expression teasing.

'I heard... I heard there's been a spy who was shot.' I pretended to concentrate on my knitting again, in case anyone should come along and see me actually talking to a trader. Then remembered it was nothing to be ashamed of and looked up at him again.

'No missy, that's not quite right,' said Xander easily. 'There was a group of envoys, I heard, from the far side of Mainland. Wanted to talk terms. They're growing a new society and think it would be in everyone's interests to join forces. They have things the Celtic Alliance needs. The Alliance has things they need... A little trading and sharing perhaps and unity against another greater enemy. But the envoys' boat was wrecked in those storms a few days back. All drowned but one. And he was a sorry wounded creature.'

'Did they shoot him?' I held my breath, thinking of the angel's golden skin and his golden hair gleaming against the rocks.

'Nay, missy. They've got him locked up somewhere nice and safe last I heard. But he's not dead. Not yet anyway. Unless those vultures in their black suits have prayed him to death. They've got a problem there. They don't want to send him back in case he takes any of their precious secrets. But they don't want to keep him forever either. A nice little dilemma for them. Why?' he grinned as he gave a sharp tug to the final strap of the tarpaulin, 'Got an interest there have you?'

'Oh no! No!' I said quickly 'Just something I heard.' I hurried away. Then I stopped and turned. 'Thank you for your help.' I said politely, not caring now who heard me.

As I went I heard him climb up and pick up the reins. Two small boys appeared from nowhere and jumped up beside him. He clicked 'Walk on!' and the horses and wagon creaked off. Gone for another six months or so. Questions were crowding my mind. How had he known Shenavar? And what adventures had she had? Oh, I wished I'd asked him!

I turned for one quick last look but the wagon was already creaking away. As if he knew I were watching, Xander turned and grinned at me and tipped his hat. I thought how easy would it be to climb up on the back of the wagon and under that tarpaulin. You could be miles away before they noticed. As far as Mainland...

Listen. *There was a small town a few miles away - houses, hotels, a youth hostel, shops and a supermarket along a river bank and the road over the bridge. Then the storms came and the bridge went and the river grew wider and washed away roads and buildings. But in the week of the great storm the sea itself roared in with waves higher than houses. It scooped up streets - rolled them up like carpets - houses, roads, the entire town and a fair few people too. Then it started on the fields and hills around. When it finally blew itself out everything had changed. We were an island. Sometimes you could see the roofs of houses, a car or a wall swirling under the waters. Then the sea would rise and foam again and sweep them all away. The mainland grew further away, vanished into the distance. And the worst thing of all was that we didn't even know if there was anyone else there left alive.'*

Chapter 8

Cabbage Breath

It wasn't quite true that the Elders had burned all Shenavar's books. Yes, they burned all those they found but they did miss one. It had slipped down the back of the shelf and because they were in such a rush to get all the books out and onto the cart - scared that Shenavar might wake up and stop them - they missed it.

When I found it jammed between the bottom of the shelf and the door frame, I hid it in a cover that said *"A Guide to Crop Diseases and Infestations for Small Cereal Growers."* which no one could get excited about. The book about crop infestations had sat all my life on the shelf in the kitchen and I don't think anyone had ever looked at it so I didn't feel even a bit bad about stealing the cover. No one even noticed.

The book I saved wasn't a story book. It was more exciting than that. It was a guide to London when it was the capital city of Great Britain and one of the most important cities in the world. London had long ago been destroyed. So in a way, I suppose, it counted as a story because that place didn't exist any more except in books.

I loved it because I could hardly believe it had ever been real. It was as different from the island as any place could be. The pictures showed entire buildings reaching up into the sky and all made of glass, the sun gleaming and glinting off them. They certainly didn't have to pull old tv sets to pieces to make those windows. There were pictures of Buckingham Palace, where the king lived, the Tower, cathedrals, huge buildings, grand houses, parks, lakes, fountains, statues and streets and streets and streets, just like Shenavar told me, full of shops full of everything you can imagine. There were theatres with dancers and singers and actors. And galleries full of pictures. Boats on the river and bridges over it. And buses and trains and cars and bikes and oh so many people...

Had the world really been like that? So *full?* So *bright?* So *sunshiney?*

I wondered what all those people did and if they lived in the grand houses and where they worked and if they strolled elegantly through those gardens or rode horses through the parks and how they spent their days. I bet they didn't have to knit wherever they went or spend so much time in church.

London has gone, of course. Father said they'd had to let it burn after the wars. So much of it had been destroyed in the bombing, so many people killed. Then when illness and starvation killed millions more there was no one left to bury them all. So they'd let the remains of the city burn and let the flames destroy the dead. Not even the traders ventured far in the city which was over-run by rats which had survived in the sewers.

Shenavar said that London had been burned to the ground before and had risen from the ashes before and she was sure it would rise up again, not in her lifetime, but maybe in mine. Maybe I would see it... I sneaked quick looks at the book, rationing myself to just one page at a time so I could drink in all the glories of it.

'Hyde Park' I said to Shenavar. 'Acres and acres of grass just growing so people can enjoy it. And boats on the lake for fun and cafes and bandstands...'

I longed to read on, but I made myself stop, to save a treat for another day. In the meantime, I hid the book under the mattress of Shenavar's bed. No one would find it there. In any case, there was other important stuff to think about.

'Last night I dreamed I was jumping out into the air and blue sky,' I told the old lady as I straightened her bed clothes and sat her up against the pillows. 'I'd misjudged the drop and I was hurtling over the rocks and to the ground. But it didn't matter. Because Fin would catch me. I couldn't see him but I knew he was there...That's what it must be like now. I can't see him, but I know he's there.'

Maybe Shenavar's misty eyes smiled in agreement. Maybe they didn't.

'The traders were asking after you Shenavar. One of them, who always looks as though he's laughing, said his grandfather knew you well. That you'd had adventures... and I should know about them...' I looked at her closely. Was there a hint of light in her eyes? This time I'm sure there was. 'I wish you'd told me about those adventures, Shenavar. Maybe one day…' Anyway, I decided not to tell her that the old man was dead. She probably couldn't hear a word I said or know who on earth I was talking about but if she did then I didn't want to make her even sadder.

'It's alright to talk to them, isn't? After all, the men do, and the likes of Callum. So why not me? There seems no good reason…' I patted her thin shoulder. 'Father was at a meeting last night. The Sharers were shouted down. He said The Elders made them seem like blasphemers. But our oil is no use to us as it is. We need men who know to make it all work. Why can't the Elders see that?'

Shenavar, of course, had always been a Sharer. If people hadn't shared what little they had - food, knowledge, shelter - the island would never have got through the hungry years and none of us would be here now. 'Father says The Elders are determined to stamp out the Sharers' ideas,' I said, as I held a cup of milk up to her mouth.

'No more stories or songs or travellers' tales now,' I said. 'I wish I could remember everything you told me. I try so hard but I can feel them slipping away. And why did the trader say I'd know more about your adventures? What did that mean?'

No answer, of course. I lifted her from the bed into the seat by the window where her bleary eyes might look across to the sea. She couldn't make it to the village baths, but I heated water on the fire and carefully washed her papery skin and kept her clean and neat. Even though the old lady had no words and mostly spent her days asleep, I knew that she appreciated it.

'Callum said there was a spy who was shot,' I told her. 'I hope it wasn't the man who looked like an angel. It wouldn't be would it? But the trader said he was an envoy not a spy. So that might be alright. Or was he a spy from the White Star states? And is there going to be another war?'

You'd think the few of us left would work together instead of killing each other. But that's not how the Elders think. What if the angel really had been a spy? Fin had rescued him so maybe they would have shot Fin too. The Elders never liked him. No they wouldn't, they couldn't…

Keep calm, calm, I told myself. Shenavar stared at me with her misty eyes.

'Fin must be near somewhere. I'll go down to the otter rocks. It's where he would come to look for me,' I said as I settled the old lady into her chair. She was a bag of sparrow bones, no effort to lift at all. I wrapped the warm shawl carefully around her shoulders. 'Right. I'll just get your medicine.'

As I went to get the medicine from the cool larder at the back of the house my mind still running on Fin and the stranger, I noticed how quiet the house was. A rare thing without children shouting or quarrelling, babies crying and Mother scolding. I stopped for a moment and relished the silence. Then Callum suddenly appeared and blocked my way.

'Callum! What are you doing home? I thought you and Father were working down at Bethel?' I tried to get past him, but he didn't move. He'd been doing this a lot lately. He thought it was clever. I thought it was really annoying. Callum was much taller than me, broad and strong. Father said he was a good worker his strength was worth two of the other lads.

'We need the heavy hammer. I've just come back for it.'

My parents had taken Callum in when my brother had gone to the Engineers. Callum was a poor swap for Davy. My brother was bright and funny and clever and kind. Callum wasn't. And he had a way of looking at me that always made me feel uncomfortable. Now Callum was of an age when he'd soon be moving out again and taking over his parents' old croft. Not soon enough as far as I was concerned.

'Well you won't find the hammer here,' I said. 'It'll be out in the barn.'

'Ah, but you're here. And all alone. I saw your mother taking the little ones to the baths and I saw Lowri way down at the bottom of the garden with the hens,' said Callum, leaning his massive arms against the wall so that I was trapped as in a cage. He stank of stale sweat and animals and yesterday's pickled cabbage, not to mention the unfamiliar sour taste of whisky. His face was lined with grime. There was no excuse for that - there was always gallons of hot water in the community baths. He just couldn't be bothered. Even though my mind was filled with thoughts of Fin, I suddenly thought of the angel, his pale beauty, his long dark eyelashes against his delicate golden skin. He would never stink of pickled cabbage.

I hated Callum so close to me. There was something... threatening about him. 'Please get out of my way,' I said firmly. 'I'm just seeing to Shenavar, then I'm off to the community centre to cook for tonight.' Not before I'd gone down to the beach again in the hope of seeing Fin. Not that I'd breathe a word of that to Callum.

Now Callum loomed over me. I wondered when he'd last cleaned his teeth. Not since he'd had the whisky, that's for sure. I was uncomfortably aware that, apart from Shenavar, I was alone in the house. 'Then there's no hurry,' leered Callum. 'You've got plenty of time. Aren't you pleased about that?' And he leaned down closer to me, as if – oh please God no – to kiss me with that vile smelling mouth.

I ducked under his arms - too close to those arm pits - and side-stepped around him. He pulled me back and with his huge raw hands clumsily tried to stroke my hair, uncovered still as I had not yet been outside and hanging loose as I tried to cling on to the memory of being on horseback with Fin. 'Get off me Callum!'

He held on to my wrist, twisting it so the skin pinched painfully. Then he looked me up and down, as if appraising a beast he was thinking of getting from a neighbour. I stamped furiously - my bare foot on his big work boot which hurt me more than him. But then I got a decent kick in on his knee. He yelped a bit but then laughed. It wasn't a pleasant laugh. I pulled myself free, twisting his wrist in the process. He glared at me angrily for a moment then grinned. 'Oh I like a lass with spirit,' he said, rubbing his wrist. Then he went off, whistling.

I ran into the kitchen, poured water into the basin and scrubbed my hands with the strong green kitchen soap to get every trace of Callum off me. And when I thought I had, I started all over again.

Listen. *'We had so many stories in our world - books, television, films. Our world was bigger and stories made it even bigger and richer.'*

Chapter 9

Discovery in the Sand

I was sure Fin would be waiting for me down at otter rocks.

But he wasn't.

No footprints, no sign of him. I sat on the smooth stone at the entrance to the cave under the overhang of the cliff. It was well hidden by large rocks so even if anyone happened to come by - and no one ever did - they wouldn't see me. There were no otters today, just the shriek of gulls and the sounds of the sea.

The tide rippled at my feet, over the rocks where I'd found the angel. Who was he? What had happened to him? Where had Fin taken him? And how? Had they really prayed over him and shot him as Callum claimed? I thought of the angel's silky hair and golden skin. I didn't want him to be dead. Not someone who seemed, even wounded and unconscious, so much more alive than so many people I knew.

Even more, I didn't want Fin dead. Even though he didn't seem like the Fin I knew. This Fin seemed harsher, more serious, as if he really were a leader. Again I wondered how had he become a member of the Elect.

I decided it must have been a joke. He'd have borrowed the horse and suit and done it all for a dare! Typical Fin! The knot in my stomach began to ease. And because he meant no harm, he'd take the horse and the clothes back to their rightful owner and come whistling into the village on foot today and nobody but us would know about it.

But what had he done with the angel stranger?

Out on the horizon I could see a boat buzzing round the rigs, a big motor boat that I knew must belong to The Engineers. No one else ventured on the oily seas. Something was going on. But what? The angel must have something to do with that. It was the best reason for him being here.

The ripples had turned and were going back out to sea now, leaving soft wet gleaming sand behind. If I stood still, I would feel my bare feet sinking deep down until I felt I'd never get out again. So I walked along the beach, keeping a look out for what had been washed ashore. The sea's currents flowed right into this little cove and often brought all sorts of interesting stuff that could prove useful.

Yes! A bright yellow plastic building brick. A whole cargo must have gone overboard at one time and they kept bobbing onto the island beaches so every child on the island had a good stock of bricks. But they always wanted more... I looked carefully. By the time I went back to the big rock where we'd once watched the otters playing, I'd found four more bricks, including one like a window, and an arm from a doll. Before I could get to it, the little plastic arm rolled back on a ripple of white surf, under the waves and back into the sea. I let it go.

Fin wasn't coming. Not today anyway. Soon it would be time for the Saturday night supper - all the villagers together in the community hall eating a big meal together. Tomorrow was the Sabbath, the Lord's Day and on the Sabbath no one cooked. Further up the beach I spotted more booty - a piece of rope, a good length of blue nylon that must have been washed up in the storm. Father would be pleased. Rope was always in short supply.

As I picked up the rope and looped it across my body, I saw something else. A shiny box. It was lying right on the high tide mark, half on wet sand, half on dry, tangled in the line of straggly seaweed. Already the wind was covering it with a drift of dry sand so it would soon disappear from view. But for now, even in the dull grey light of the overcast day, it gleamed.

It was a strange box, made of smooth silvery metal, about two foot square and about three inches deep. Not particularly heavy, I thought, as I picked it up and turned it over. Very scratched and battered with a sizeable dent on the side. It had a sheen on it but no really thick oil, so couldn't have been long in the water. I could see that it was meant open but the dent was jamming the lock so I couldn't manage it.

There was some tiny writing pressed into one corner. *Sat.com* it said, which meant nothing at all to me. Maybe it was English. Or even another language. I found this idea exciting. Wherever it came from, whatever it was for, it wasn't far from where I'd found the angel. Perhaps it was something to do with him.

Fin would know what to do. When I saw him I would tell him about it. For now, I carried the box up to the cave where the sea rarely reached and placed it on a dry ledge and wedged it in with pebbles to stop it slipping. Then I covered it with more pebbles. No one would find it. It was safe for now.

Listen. '*Our computers were useless. We'd relied on them for everything but with no power and no internet they were soon hopeless. Our only knowledge was in books and we rescued all we could find that could teach us things – about animals, farming, making medicines – to keep our bodies alive. But we needed the books of stories too, of poetry and plays. They fed our souls. They helped us dream. Without dreams, there's no point in going on.*'

Chapter 10

Shock at Supper

'Where've you been?' asked Bekah, rushing towards me as soon as I came in 'Have you seen? Have you heard...?'

'You girls!' the voice of Mrs Chief Elder rang out. 'Stop gossiping and get on with your work! Bekah – take these plates through to the hall. Now!'

As Bekah scuttled into the hall, she was pink with excitement, looking back over her shoulder to me, trying to tell me something without actually speaking but I couldn't make it out, especially not with Mrs Chief Elder breathing like a dragon down my neck.

'Oh Amity,' said Priscilla sweetly, sidling up to me, making sure her grandmother could hear. 'Where have you been? You've been *such* a long time! It must have been something *very* important to keep you so long. We didn't think you were going to do any work at all today!'

I glared at her. Mrs Chief Elder glared at me.

Luckily someone asked her something so I turned back to work. As Mrs Chief Elder watched, I went straight to the big sink, washed pots, laid the long tables, set out jugs of water, carried dishes, pans, knives, forks, roasting trays… Why did we have to eat altogether like this?

Although we had electricity on the island - thanks to the wind turbines - to have it in private houses would be a wasteful extravagance of God's resources that led to idleness and sin. Well, that's what the Elders said. They believed in communal living and thought that people were happier doing things together. Probably just so they could keep an eye on us. So we only had peat fires to cook on at home but big electric ovens and ranges in the community centre. This was why the big Saturday meal was a communal affair with all the women preparing it together.

Long ago Shenavar told me stories of preparing food on her own small cooker in her own little kitchen, a meal for a boyfriend. That sounded sort of nice. Just the two of them. Simple - and impossible on the island. Oh! I suddenly remembered, I'd forgotten to give Shenavar her medicine! I'd been so busy avoiding Callum. Too late now. I'd do it later.

'Amity,' hissed Bekah, who's managed to squeeze in right next to me as we took the last jugs of water into the hall and put them on the tables, 'Have you seen…?'

But the Elders were coming in. We had to scamper back to our places. There was a shuffling silence as everyone in the room got on their feet to say Grace. As the Elders strode up to the big table at the head of the hall there was a newcomer among them –

someone tall and young with close-cropped curls. A rustle rippled all around the room as people realised who he was.

Bekah looked triumphantly at me. This was what she'd been trying to tell me. Fin was back... I took a deep breath, determined to keep calm, look cool. Fin. He was here. It hadn't been a joke. There he was dressed as one of The Elect walking up to the top table. But at least he was alive and hadn't been shot.

In daylight, even at the far end of the room, I could see the changes I'd noted in him in the twilight days before. He seemed taller, older – a lot older than just the two years that had passed since I'd seen him. Walking down the hall in his black suit he looked serious, weighed down as if he were trying not to burst into a Fin leap or jump. He must be just pretending to be so grown up.

I gazed at him, drilled my thoughts into the back of his head, willing him to turn round and grin at me the way he always used to. Instead he walked steadily on. What's more, The Elders, who were all at least three times his age and had known him since he a was a little crawling baby, who'd spent years trying to beat the Devil out of him, were now giving way to him. What?

Priscilla looked smug. She must have known already, of course. But no one else did. I heard the small surprised intake of breath around the room, the suppressed buzz of astonishment. Fin Williams, well remembered as being a rebellious boy, a troublesome teenager, out of his sister's control and in sore need of God's good guidance was back home and one of The Elect? The rest of the villagers were even more surprised than I was.

'God moves in mysterious ways, right enough,' muttered an old woman at the end of the row.

'A time of miracles and wonders indeed,' said another, raising her eyes to heaven.

Fin bowed gravely to them all and took his place at the head of the table. I was still waiting for the sideways glance, the quick grin. It didn't come. Instead though, Bekah was still nudging me so furiously that I was forced to step away a little from her.

Fin stood quietly looking around the room, demanding silence by the sheer force of his presence. The crowds crammed around the waiting tables gradually shushed and looked up at him. Then Fin, in a measured, powerful voice said Grace, a duty normally done by the Chief Elder who today just stood by Fin's side, apparently content to take second place. At the end the whole room almost shouted the last 'Amen' in relief to their pent-up astonishment at this strange turn of affairs.

Then all the women come bustling out to dish out the food to the waiting men folk. I couldn't serve Fin and The Elders – that was an honour given to the older married women, so I couldn't even get near. By the time all the men had been served and we women sat by ourselves at the tables at the bottom end of the hall, I was so far away that I could barely see Fin through the crowd.

I was craning my neck to see him when Mother rapped me across the knuckles with a spoon. 'Stop gawping, girl and eat the good food the Lord has provided!'

Fin, deep in serious conversation with The Elders, didn't even glance in my direction. I barely tasted the food in front of me, as I churned over what had happened to my laughing rebel Fin. At the end of the meal and after the long grace of thanksgiving, Fin led the Elders out of the hall. All the women curtseyed as the men walked past. As Fin drew level with me, I lifted my head and gazed straight at him. He looked back. For a moment I thought I saw a glint of something, of affection maybe. But no. I must have imagined it. His stern expression gave no flicker of recognition, let alone love. Then he looked quite deliberately away and walked on.

I wrapped my fingers around the little wooden otter in my pocket, so hard I thought I'd break it.

Back home, Callum was more objectionable than ever. 'Yon Fin's gone terribly grand now, hasn't he?' he taunted, 'No time for the likes of you, Amity. He hardly even looked at you. And,' he said coming up too close, in a particularly sneering tone, 'you were always such *special* friends.'

I whipped round to shout at him but Father interrupted. 'Leave the lass alone, Callum,' he said in his slow strong voice. 'Fin was a special friend of us all. He and Davy were like puppies from the same litter, always together. He was always in and out of this house and always welcome, long before you came to live here.'

I gave Father a quick, grateful glance. 'I'll see to Shenavar,' I said, taking a small dish of supper for the old lady. In the quiet safety of the old lady's room I helped Shenavar eat and told her all about the scenes in the supper room. 'He looked away from me so deliberately!' I said. 'As if there was never anything between us. As if..'

Shenavar turned her head towards me, almost as if

she wanted to say something but there was no chance. It was a long time since Shenavar had spoken. To make up for the medicine she'd missed, I tried to give her a double dose. But when I approached her with the spoon the old lady turned her head away. Not once but twice. There was something so determined about her actions that I couldn't force her. Maybe one day wouldn't matter. I'd try again in the morning.

I could hear sounds of conversation as they gathered around the fire in the family room. I didn't want to put up with the odious Callum going on about Fin. I didn't understand what had happened and it hurt my head to think. Instead, I curled the rug against the door, so it would jam when anyone tried to open it. I settled Shenavar comfortably and then I sat and tried to tell myself one of the stories she'd told me when I was little. About the poor boy who defeated the giant, or the clever girl who outwitted the wicked sorcerer. 'You always have to think for yourself' she told me then. 'There's nearly always a way out.'

Listen. 'When the storms finally blew over we were in a different world. So much had been destroyed, torn away, smashed against the rocks. So many people had died. We who were left were battered and bruised, damaged and dizzy with shock. Then Meic Morgan —your friend Bekah's great grandfather – found a flute. Someone had a guitar with nearly all its strings and someone else a mouth organ. That night we made a fire and sat round it making music and singing. It wasn't great music or great singing but it gave us courage to face the dark and the future.'

Chapter 11

The Shaming

'**R**ight, Amity. You can do the milking today. I don't know where you were yesterday but I don't think you did your fair share of work towards the Saturday feast,' said Mother, shaking me awake on Sabbath morning.

I didn't think she'd noticed I'd been late to the kitchens. I should have realised, Mother notices *everything*. She went downstairs to feed baby Liam and I got dressed in my work clothes, wrapped an old sacking apron around me and took a bucket out to the cows. She still hadn't forgiven me for turning down Idris Mordecai. 'You think you can pick and choose, my girl. Well let's hope you can. You should have a home of your own now and a baby or two to keep you out of trouble and stop your wandering ways.'

She went on and on, 'Your father and I took you in when you were a poor orphan child. And is this the thanks we get for our Christian charity? A great lump of a girl who's going to eat us out of house and home for ever and shame me in front of everyone. All those mothers who have daughters giving them fine grandchildren to people the world and take God's word forwards. And what do I have? A girl who's never there when she's wanted and is in a dream when she is.' It was a constant irritating buzz in my ear, like a fly in the room. I did my best to ignore it, bit my tongue and didn't answer back.

Anyway, I knew Mother didn't really grudge the food - we had plenty. And I don't really mind the milking. We have just two cows, small docile creatures who let me lean my head against them as I milk them. By the time I'd finished Elspeth and Morag were feeding the hens. Bryn had fed the pig. The only work we did on the Sabbath was what was necessary for the animals. Everything else had to wait. On the Sabbath we concentrated on God. Then we all went in and got washed and changed into Sunday best, including boots. We never went barefoot to church, not even in summer.

'Iolo! Put your shoes back on! Jamie! Pull your socks up!' Mother was having a final inspection of us all. She wiped Erin's face, made Bryn wash his hands. 'Right, you'll do,' she said.

Here we all were, ready, faces scrubbed, hair brushed, in Sunday clothes. Everyone made an effort. We had blazers bought years before from the Traders. Once they had been part of a school uniform (Imagine having special clothes for school!) and might have been quite smart but were now worn and faded, even though kept for best. They said *King's Academy* on the pocket. Mine had a nametape inside that said *Lucy Stevenson* in curly writing. I wondered about Lucy Stevenson, who she was and what had happened to her...

Our feet squashed into boots that the boys had

polished the night before. Or into trainers that we had to scrub to keep white. My feet were particularly squashed because I was still growing and because I was now the eldest, I had no one above from whom to inherit a bigger size.

Mother was wearing a coat so worn it was almost like gossamer but clean and decent and well cut. She also had her hat. It was a big black hat, very fragile that had once belonged to her grandmother. We haven't been able to get hats like that since the wars so women who still had them treasured them. Mother's hat had once had a big bow on it but she'd taken it off because she considered it too frivolous. I think it would have looked nice with a bow.

We set off. Father at the front carrying baby Liam, Mother leading little Erin by the hand. Then came Callum with Iolo and Bryn, followed by Elspeth and the twins, Charity and Morag and little Petroc. Lowri and I came last so we could keep an eye on the little ones.

'Do you think Fin will be there?' whispered Lowri, as I grabbed Petroc to stop him from jumping in a puddle. I shrugged. I didn't know which would be worse – if he wasn't there, or if he was there and didn't speak to me, as he'd done the night before. As I re-tied Petroc's bootlace for him, I realised my insides were also tied into a tight, tense knot. I'm sorry God, it wasn't the best way to go to church but I couldn't help it.

All over the village there were similar family groups, all scrubbed and polished and dressed up in what passed for Sunday best, little processions of parents with anything up to fourteen children making their way to the church. Ours was a big family but wasn't unusual or the biggest. That was another thing the Elders were always quoting 'Like arrows in the hands of warriors are children born in in one's youth. Blessed is the man whose quiver is full of them.'

OK, we needed to re-stock the world with people, but the man wasn't the one giving birth every year, was he? But that was something else I didn't dare say out loud.

'Look!' said Lowri suddenly, 'There's the Blackwoods.'

'So it is,' I replied, surprised at this sudden enthusiasm for our neighbours. The Blackwoods were now walking parallel to us about twenty yards away. There were seven children and when the oldest darted a quick look towards Lowri - aha!- I understood her sudden interest.

Cornelius Blackwood was a good-looking lad with sandy hair and freckles, tall and slim. Although he was certainly bright enough to join the Engineers the Elders had decided he should stay on the island as he had a way with animals, a skill at setting bones and dealing with difficult births in cows. He had a knack that no one else had of talking to them almost, that calmed them down. Of course he and Lowri were two of a kind.

I grinned at my sister. 'So that's how it is!' I said. 'Well, he's a fine lad.'

Lowri blushed. I looked across at Cornelius and he blushed too. I hoped it would turn out well for them.

'Oh and look!' said Lowri, still blushing at a glance from Cornelius, 'there's Idris Mordecai talking to Cornelius's sister Hannah.'

Hannah was very sweet but a bit slow and simple. Lowri and I looked at each other 'Perfect!' we agreed.

'Still,' I muttered, 'He might have stayed a bit

heartbroken a bit longer after I'd turned him down instead of dashing straight off to find himself a wife.. And from me to…Hannnah…'

'Baa,' whispered Lowri and we started to giggle.

'Girls!' snapped Mother. 'Stop that unseemly behaviour at once! What will people think and on the Sabbath too.'

We walked on, stifling our giggles. Just before we got to the village centre, Mother turned to us. 'Now remember, there's a Shaming today. Behave yourselves. And you girls, watch and learn and remember. You don't want to end up like Lizzie.'

That stopped our laughter.

'I hate Shamings,' I said under my breath to Lowri. 'I never know where to look.'

'I know,' muttered Lowri. 'The people being shamed are so sad and the ones watching are so smug – as if they've never done anything wrong in their lives!'

'It must be Lizzie Llewellyn today, on account of her baby. She never said who the father is…'

'They said the Elders beat her to get her to give his name. But she'd still refused,' said Lowri. 'Do you think they did?'

'I'm sure of it,' I said grimly. 'When they're pursuing sin there's nothing will stop them, not even a young girl going to have a baby.'

'I don't want to watch,' said Lowri.

'Close your eyes and think of something else,' I said, knowing it wouldn't be as easy as that.

At the church door, Father handed baby Liam over to Mother and he and Callum and the boys went in one door and sat downstairs, while Lowri, Ellen, Elspeth, Morag and I trudged up the stairs with Mother, Erin and the baby to sit in the gallery with the other women and children.

'Is that Fin down there?' whispered Lowri. 'Sitting with the Elders?' I nodded.

I could just see the top of his head. But I could tell by the set of his shoulders that he was nervous. Maybe he didn't want to watch a Shaming either.

Listen. *'Before the wars on Mainland and all over the world there used to be beautiful churches, huge buildings with carving and statues and flowers and incense that filled the space with wonderful smells and stained glass that filled it with dancing colour.'*

Our church wasn't like that. No coloured glass. No statues. No pictures. No flowers. Just the grey light of a grey day. Absolutely plain with nothing to look at, at all. And of course no music. That was the idea. You weren't supposed to be distracted. You were supposed to spend all your time thinking of God.

Normally I tried. But today, when I dragged my eyes off Fin, I was looking at the men below me. One of them was no doubt the father of Lizzie's child, probably already married which is why he couldn't marry Lizzie. The Elders knew. Of course they did. But they would still say it was Lizzie's fault for enticing a married men, that men are weak and women are evil. So Lizzie had to make her way the entire length of the church on her knees, while carrying her baby.

Sometimes her skirts got caught under her and she had to shift the baby to try and untangle them. The baby was only six weeks old. Lizzie looked exhausted but the Elders didn't care about that. They didn't care when the baby wailed and when Lizzie sobbed. You could see it was really painful and uncomfortable for her to go all that way on the knees. I never realised the church was so long...

The Elders kept telling us we had to be without sin to keep close to God because we were the Chosen People. But did God really want poor Lizzie and her baby to be so wretched? Lizzie's mother and grandmother sat near us, mouths clamped shut like metal traps, looking straight ahead with tears rolling silently down their cheeks. Whether for pity or shame I couldn't tell. Lowri had her eyes closed. A few of the congregation looked embarrassed. Father was gazing up at the ceiling. Some tried not to stare. But most looked smugly at poor Lizzie. Maybe seeing her suffer made them feel better. That included some of the girls I knew had babies on the way before they made it to church for a wedding. You could see that they thought they were better than Lizzie.

Lizzie was being allowed to keep her baby but she would be sent as housekeeper to old Angus Morgan. He lived at the far end of the island with his two sons who were grown up but simple minded and would never marry so they had no woman in the house. I shuddered. It would be no easy life.

The Chief Elder towered above Lizzie and talked of sin and harlotry and hell and the devil until Lizzie was frightened out of her wits, reduced to hysterical sobbing. The baby was purple with wailing and no one could hear anything. Then Mrs Deputy Chief Elder came forward and, almost kindly, lifted Lizzie to her feet, took the baby from her and led her out. It was the first touch of humanity I'd seen in that church. We could hear the wails fading in the distance, which was a relief. There was a short uncomfortable silence which gave us all time to fidget and soothe the children who'd started wailing in sympathy with Lizzie's baby as we waited for the Chief Elder to preach.

Only he didn't. Instead it was Fin in his black suit with the silk collar who stood up and walked to the front. He stood quietly for a moment, looking around him, his eyes raking around the men downstairs - and maybe he lingered for a second longer on Maldwyn MacArthur whom I'd once seen talking very closely with Lizzie - and then he looked up to the women and children in the gallery, a long cool stare.

'Brothers and sisters!' he said. 'The fires of Hell are waiting for you!' Some people blinked a little. But Fin had only started.

I couldn't believe it. Nobody could. He preached for an hour or more, promising the hope of Heaven for the Chosen and the promise of hellfire and damnation for those who strayed. And how we should strive harder, look into our consciences, and bring ourselves closer to God. He stirred people up, so much so that Elspeth snuggled up next to me with her thumb in her mouth and Mother didn't even frown.

'Amen!' people shouted sometimes. And 'Halleluia!' and 'Save us Lord!' People began to sway, as if he was hypnotising them.

I had to pinch myself to remind me that this was Fin - Fin, who used to laugh and mock at everything. Fin who loved Shenavar's stories as much as I did. Fin who'd never agreed with the Elders but who wanted to make links and share with Outland. Fin, whom I could trust to catch me when I launched myself out off a rock. And here he was, with the entire congregation listening intently to his every word.

Part of me admired it - it was an amazing performance - but otherwise I was horrified. This was the opposite of what Fin had ever said or thought or shared with me. What had happened? I remembered lying wrapped in his arms on the white sand. Of how close we were then, his arms around me in love and sunshine. And I wondered how he could stand there and join in this condemnation of Lizzie.

Sometimes he even used some of the Chief Elder's favourite phrases. 'We must be *brrrands* plucked from the *burrrrning*' with the long rolling 'r' that he had always mocked so vividly as he posed, arms outstretched on top of the otter rock. But there was no mockery in his eyes in church, just religious fervour. Fin had been born again into God's light and had no need of me. Nor I of him.

That night I dreamed I was jumping off the rock again, into the sky, soaring alone into nothingness.

Chapter 12

A Monday Morning Visit

'Who'd have thought that young scamp would turn out be such a fine strong preacher?' said Mother on Monday morning as she doled out bowls of porridge for everyone and bacon for the men, all the time with baby Liam swaddled on her hip.

'Aye,' replied Father, who'd already done an hour's work and smelt of cold fresh air and muddy boots. 'There are miracles indeed, signs and wonders in these strange days.'

Callum, snatching an extra slice of thick fat bacon mumbled through a mouth full of food 'He always made fun of the minister and now they're all looking up to him. How did he do that? You were always thick with him Amity, don't you know anything?'

I too had already been out in the chilly morning to milk the cows again. I dumped my heavy sacking apron in the back kitchen and came through with the bucket of warm milk to give the children some, nearly tripping over Nutmeg who'd sneaked into the house, following Father.

Dr John had sent for Lowri to come and help him with a tricky operation on young Charlie Jones's broken leg. Since Davy left the island, said Dr John, Lowri was the only person with enough common sense and composure to stay calm and be useful when the blood was flowing. Some of the women thought that it wasn't right for a young girl to do things like that but as they were all busy with their husbands and families they were glad enough for someone else to help the doctor. Still, maybe Lowri might find a way of accidentally bumping into Cornelius Blackwood between Dr John's house and ours…

Erin was screaming like a stuck pig and Iolo was chasing her. I grabbed Erin's foot and hauled her out of danger. There is never peace in our house, only in Shenavar's tiny room. I ran my fingers automatically over the little carved wooden otter in my pocket. It gave me no comfort. Like the wet sand sinking away under me and then vanishing in the incoming tide, all the things I'd been sure of made no sense any more.

Erin was still squealing and the twins Charity and Morag were protesting as I brushed their hair and put it in plaits ready for school 'Ow, Amity you're *tugging!*' when there was a brisk knock, the door opened, Nutmeg barked joyously and suddenly the room was filled with Fin's presence.

It was so strange, the boy who'd spent half his life in this same house now seemed somehow to command it. He strode in, stepping neatly over Liam and Erin, shook hands with Father, nodded at Callum and walked over to Mother who was already curtseying to him – as if she'd never chased him and

Davy out with the broom so many times when they were young. I gazed with my jaw dropping but Fin wasn't looking at me, instead he was talking to my parents. 'I couldn't leave without seeing you and giving you what tidings I have of Davy,' he said as both parents looked eagerly towards him. 'True it's some time since I've seen him but word comes that he's doing well, he's well thought of and has completed his medical studies.'

'Completed?' interrupted Father, 'So soon?'

'These are difficult times, sir. We must seize the day if we are to achieve God's plan. And if what we hear is right, then we might sadly have need of as many doctors as we can.'

I only vaguely heard what Fin had said about Davy. Here was Fin – rebellious, mocking Fin - sounding just like one of the fusty old Elders. I was still trying to catch up with what he said. I coughed. 'Did you say you're leaving?' I asked, trying to make my voice sound normal, casual, and, despite Mother's pointed frowns, absolutely not curtseying, as I fixed the final tie on Charity's plaits.

Fin looked straight at me. 'I am,' he said. 'God's work brought me here and now He takes me away. There have been,' he paused, 'a few problems to deal with.'

Yes, I thought, an angel with a broken arm washed up by the sea for a start.

'… but they have been dealt with, so now I am free to go.'

'Dealt with satisfactorily?' I asked, still looking at Charity's hair. He would know I was asking about the angel.

'Yes,' said Fin. 'For now.'

'Will you be back soon?'

'It's in God's hands but probably not.' He sounded almost off hand, as if it were no importance to him. 'I am in no position to make promises. You understand.' He gazed directly into my eyes, his grey eyes as hard as flint, as if trying to force the words directly into my head. 'I can make no promises at all.'

'I understand,' I said coldly, getting the message all too clearly. I had trusted him on his promise as I'd trusted him to catch me when I launched myself out into the open sky.

'This is no time for promises,' said Fin again. Mother, Father and Callum watched us, saying nothing. Fin held my gaze for a second longer and then looked down at my skirt where there was a splash of cow muck from when I'd been doing the milking. 'Remember, Amity, that cleanliness is next to godliness,' he said sternly.

What! 'How dare you! Did you really say that?' I turned on him. 'Are you saying there's something ungodly about good honest cow muck from good honest work? Are you so grand now that...'

'Amity!' said my mother, grabbing my arm. 'Stop that now!'

'I'm so sorry, Fin, sir,' she went on - apologising to Fin! - 'The girl has no right to speak to you like that.'

'But..!' I started and caught Father's warning expression. For a second, I thought I saw a gleam in Fin's eyes. But as he turned away from me and carried on talking to my parents, I realised I must have imagined it. I closed my mouth, speechless with indignation at his patronising attitude. How dare he!

Then Fin made his farewells. 'Goodbye Amity,' he said and suddenly his eyes seemed full of sadness.

Now he looked so old. Then he seemed to pull himself together and strode smartly out. All the children tumbled out through the door behind him to see the horse – the same horse that I'd ridden just a few days ago. Fin jumped up on it and the horse trotted down the street, taking him out of the village, off the island and out of my life. I didn't even go to the door to look. After the way he'd changed so much, I could hardly be sad he was going.

So now, after two years waiting, finding him so changed made me raw with disappointment. But even more, I was so angry with him! How could he have changed so much? How *dare* he speak to me like that?

Listen. *'And the handsome prince pulled his sword out of the dead dragon and rushed to untie the princess who had been about to become the dragon's breakfast. Her dress was only slightly burned and her crown only slightly wonky. The prince gazed into her eyes and fell in love with her beauty, despite the smoky smudges on her face. They married and lived happily ever after.*

On the other hand. Wouldn't it have been much better if the princess had been taught a bit of dragon-fighting herself? Then she wouldn't have to hang around getting slowly toasted in the hope of some handsome prince just happening to pass by. Handsome princes are, of course, wonderful. But it's always better, Amity, if you can kill your own dragons…'

Chapter 13

Sparkly Shoes

'Alright,' I said as I went in to an awkward little silence. 'I can tell you've been talking about me.'

I'd gone round to Susannah's. Even Mother hadn't thought to stop me.

'Has he gone?' asked Bekah sympathetically. She was already there, cuddling the baby, of course.

I nodded. How many times had I boasted that when Fin came back we would leave the island together? And now he'd come and gone and I was still here. Bekah was just too nice to say anything nasty or 'I told you so,' to me. I hope she and Davy did get together. She would be so good to him.

'Horse!' said little Lachlan, jumping up and down. 'I saw horse!'

'We saw him go past,' said Susannah, apologetically, stroking Lachlan's head. There was another awkward silence.

'He just seemed a different person,' I said

hopelessly. 'I don't know what's happened.' I sat on the floor and Lachlan clambered on to me. I found his toy bricks and started building him a tower. He knocked it down. I built it up again. This could go on for hours. The same pointless thing over and over again. That's island life.

'It's happened before,' said Susannah. 'Lots of times. There's always stories of wicked hard-drinking, loose-living men who repented their ways and found a new life filled with God. They're always the most zealous, the newly converted, like Euan's uncle Gareth.'

'But not like Fin,' I said.

'No perhaps not like Fin. But you know Amity, he was always so very clever and you never knew what he was going to do next.'

'He always did the most unexpected thing, didn't he?' said Susannah. 'And you have to admit this is the most unexpected thing he could ever do. Even for Fin.'

That almost - almost - made me smile. 'Do you think he really meant it?' I asked, willing them to say no.

Bekah and Susannah looked at each other. 'It looked pretty convincing to me,' said Susannah. 'He was a powerfully good preacher. He must have been doing it for a long time. He must be good to be one of the Elect. He must be the youngest ever.'

I nodded gloomily, tossing the little wooden bricks back and for in my hands until Lachlan grabbed them and demanded another tower. There was no doubt. The Fin I thought I knew had gone. I was on my own now. The sympathetic looks from Bekah and Susannah made that all too clear.

'Lizzie Llewellyn has gone to Angus Morgan's,' said Bekah suddenly to break the silence. 'I saw her going with the baby. But her brother was going with her, carrying her bag. He'll have words with the Morgans no doubt. Make sure they treat her properly.'

Nevertheless, we all shivered at the thought of the sort of life Lizzie would have with the Morgan men and were plunged even further into gloom. Then Bekah, always ready to cheer us up, whispered 'Susannah, could we look at the shoes?'

Cautiously, Susannah looked out through the tiny window.

'There's no one around,' said Bekah. 'And the boys will be alright playing for a while. Please? It's such a long time since we looked at them.'

'Come on then,' said Susannah, grinning.

We crept upstairs and into Susannah's bedroom. 'Here, take the baby,' she said to me. Then moving the small crib that blocked the big cupboard door, she reached right into the back and produced a faded box. She placed it reverently on the bed and removed the lid.

'There…' And, as always, we gasped.

'We will never, ever have shoes like that,' sighed Bekah.

They were scarlet – a rich, bold, vivid scarlet that made the workaday blankets and rug in Susannah's bedroom seem even more faded and shabby than usual. Those shoes lit up the room. They sparkled with hundreds of tiny beads across the narrow toes. They fastened with the narrowest strap with more beads and a small bow. But the heels….!

Instead of clumpy flat heels like our Sunday boots these had tall, thin, elegant heels, nearly five inches high, narrow and dainty. We gazed at them, filling our eyes with the sight. 'Imagine a world which had those shoes in it,' I said. 'Just think what it would be like.'

I handed the baby back to Susannah and Bekah

and I each gently picked a shoe from the box and held it in our hands, turning it over and admiring it. 'Remember when we used to try them on and go tottering across the room?' asked Bekah. 'We always collapsed in a heap. We could have broken them.' She looked horrified at the thought. Now we didn't dare risk breaking those narrow, lethal heels. 'I couldn't bear it if we spoilt them.'

The shoes had belonged to Susannah's great-grandmother, a friend of Shenavar's. Somehow the shoes had survived the wars, fires, floods and black clouds. Anything useful on the island long been salvaged and used for something else. Anything decorative had been bargained with the traders years ago. Or destroyed by the Elders. But the shoes had somehow survived, a relic of another world.

'Do you remember the trousers?' asked Bekah.

'Ooh yes,' said Susannah. 'They were a bit revealing, weren't they? They clung to our skin. They weren't like the trousers the lads wear now.' We all thought about the trousers for a moment. Trousers meant for girls.

'I'd never have dared go out in them,' giggled Bekah, 'Not when people might see…'

'Ah well, we never got the chance. Not after my mother came in.'

Susannah's mother had come in one day when it was Susannah's turn to try on the trousers. Susannah had been standing with one hand on her hip, her long hair loose around her shoulders, looking like an old photo we'd once found of her great granny. Her mother had been furious and yanked the trousers so hard off Susannah that they'd been ripped. Then she slapped Susannah's legs and called us all shameless hussies. Bekah, near to tears but very dignified had said 'We're not hussies. We're just interested.' Susannah's mother wasn't impressed and shooed and slapped us all out of the house.

The trousers had long since been turned into clothes for small boys. But I still remembered striding around the room in them, the amazing sense of lightness and freedom after our long thick bulky skirts.

I took one last look at the shoes, dreaming what it must have been like to wear such shoes, dance in them, wearing the dresses that Shenavar had described, listening to music I could only imagine. We all sighed, then reluctantly we put the shoes away. Susannah hid the box at the back of the cupboard, pushed the cot back in place and we went downstairs again to see what havoc the boys were causing, back in our unchanging grey world.

Then I had something I had to do.

The sea was grey and choppy and rain squalled around as I wrapped my shawl more tightly around me. My heart was sinking as I took the little carved otter from my pocket, held it to my lips and kissed it for one last time.

'I mean nothing to Fin any more so you mean nothing to me,' I told it, remembering the chill in Fin's eyes. 'You're nothing more than just a clever bit of wood. I was a fool for clinging to you for so long. Goodbye Fin!' I yelled into the wind and rain.

I whipped my arm right back and hurled the tiny carving towards the sea. It soared up against the grey sky, fell and vanished, swallowed up by the torrent of spray from the crashing waves. I turned my back on the sea, the otter and on Fin and walked up the beach.

Now I was the only one who could sort out my future.

Then I nearly fell over a small rowing boat. It was pulled up between the rocks as though to hide it from view. Unusual. Rocks and roaring currents had smashed most of our small craft. There weren't many boats left on the island but this must have been here for a day at least because the tide had washed any footprints away. Strange.

Wondering who had brought this boat here and where they were now, I wandered the beach, automatically looking to see what had been washed up. I pounced on a piece of wood, well bashed by the waves but still useful. What's more it had a few nails in the end. Nails were always in short supply. There was a plastic carrier bag too, blowing across the sand. Excellent. I stopped it with my foot. They're good for so many things but especially for blocking up broken windows. And there was the doll's arm again, washed back in from the sea onto this patch of sand. This time I picked it up and put it in my pocket. There'll always be a doll in need of an arm.

But there was no sign of anyone who might have come in the boat.

The wind had dropped a little. I trailed the wood alongside me so it left a little pattern in the sand among the pockmarked pits and ripples the rain had left behind. Then I looked into the cave. No one there. I went in and checked the ledge at the back where the *sat.com* box was still hidden by pebbles and undisturbed.

As I came out of the darkness and into the daylight I blinked and just for a fraction of a second I saw a sudden gleam of gold. Then it vanished behind tall dark rocks where a steep slope fell down from the fields above. I dropped the wood and ran across, calling out, as I scrambled over the rocks and down the other side, to the wide boggy mouth of a stream. Three cormorants squawked up into the air in alarm, their huge wings flapping and an otter slithered off a rock and into the water.

I stopped, looked. I could see no one. But I was sure someone was there. I was sure I hadn't imagined it. I took one more long look around me, picked up the wood then walked back to the village. As I came to the sandy path up from the shoreline, Callum appeared from nowhere and started walking beside me. 'So where you've been?' he asked suspiciously.

'Beachcombing for Father,' I said, 'Look, I've found some nails.'

Callum moved too close to me and I stepped away. Then he would get closer again and I would wave the length of wood and move away again. In this strange fashion we made our way home. I just hoped no one thought we were actually walking together.

Still, I was wondering who had been down on the beach. It had to be someone who had arrived in a small boat, someone who'd disturbed the birds and the otter. Someone with gleaming gold hair, who didn't want to be seen.

Listen. *'If we ever got a clear day we could still just see the mainland far across the waters. When we saw smoke we knew at last that we weren't alone. We tried to get to them but the rocks and currents were treacherous. Boats and people smashed like matchwood. Three young men drowned. They were our bravest, brightest and best. After that we said no more attempts with boats. We had no young people to spare.'*

91

Chapter 14

Gunfire

'Thunder,' said Father, looking up at the sound as he and Callum heaved a big stone into the cart. 'Strange. It doesn't seem a thundery day.' They piled two more stones in the cart and Father stood up and stretched his back. 'Time for a break.'

They were taking stone from a long abandoned house on the cliff top and bringing it back to build a bigger pen for our sheep. There'd been a tractor to do that sort of work once and a small fuel allowance. But the tractor had broken down and there was no spare part for it and it was many years since anyone but the Engineers had any of our precious fuel. So the tractor lay on its side, rusting behind a barn with nettles growing over it. Soon no one will know that it's there.

'Here, have some milk,' I said, offering them the can I'd just brought up the hill for them. 'And here's some oatcakes and salt mutton.'

Father and Callum sat down on the half

92

demolished wall, taking it in turns to drink from the can. I perched on the sheltered edge of the cart, out of the way of the wind. Absent-mindedly I tickled Nutmeg's ears and looked at the nettles and brambles growing through walls of what had been someone's house. In the corners you could still see the faded scraps of flowery wall paper. I wondered about the people who'd chosen that paper and put it up however many years ago. Did they have shops where they bought wallpaper or had they ordered it on their computers, or even their phones as Shenavar said you could? And how could you do that?

There was another rumble. 'They're getting a storm on Mainland,' said Callum, sounding cheerful of course because someone else was suffering. Sure enough, we saw the quick flashes of light along the horizon.

'Odd,' said Father. 'The air is fresh and clear. Not stormy weather. And I can see no clouds over there.' Then we heard the rumbles again. This time the light flashed at the same time. Not bright and white but ragged and red and yellow.

'Funny lightning,' said Callum, jumping off the wall and going to the cliff edge to get a closer look. 'It seems to be coming up from the ground, not down from the sky.' Father put the milk can down on the wall and gazed across to Mainland, his expression stern. 'That's not lightning,' he said. 'It's gunfire. Near the refinery. Someone's attacking Mainland.'

The church was full that night. Everyone flocked in. We'd all seen the gun fire, heard the explosions. We knew that the enemy, whoever that might be, was getting closer.

As everyone fluttered and panicked and restless

children cried, the Elders led us in an hour of prayers. We were exhorted to be true to God, to walk the paths of righteousness, to make ourselves worthy. 'We must scrub sin from our hearts, from our very thoughts.'

Then, when our knees were aching from kneeling and our throats sore from shouting 'Amen!' the Elders told us what was happening. This was a new threat, they said, from the White Star states in the north and east. They were trying to take the old refineries, get access to the Mainland oil reserves. The Elders weren't sure yet – news took time to travel – but didn't think they had succeeded. 'But they will surely keep trying! They want our oil rigs, the oil God entrusted to us.'

'They must not triumph!' declaimed the Chief Elder. 'God's gift for The Chosen must be guarded for God's purpose,' he said, banging the pulpit in front of him. 'The godless must not benefit!' He said the Engineers would be coming soon to guard the island. 'In the meantime, we must look after ourselves. We shall be organising our own patrols. Every able-bodied man will get more cartridges for their shot guns. A number will also get rifles. We must protect our own. And our most important duty is to keep faith and be worthy of His protection.'

Then there was another hour of prayer.

As we left church, some of the babies and small children asleep in their parents' arms, we came out into a clear evening, the sky a mass of stars twinkling above us. Such clearness, the lack of oily clouds, would normally cheer us up. Not tonight. Despite the lateness of the hour and the chill of the breeze, people stood in small groups wanting to talk. Quietly

I crept around little huddles of people sharing their woes and worries until I was next to Fin's sister Hepzibah. A lot older than Fin, she was newly married when their parents died and had taken him in as a toddler. She soon had a house full of children of her own which is why Fin had more freedom than many island children and why he'd spent so much time in our house.

I liked Hepzibah. She was large and smiley and gentle, despite the houseful of children. Her youngest baby was asleep in the shawl wrapped around her, two or three other children clung to her skirts.

'Hello Amity' she said, then paused. 'Did you see Fin at all?'

'Not really,' I said. 'Not to talk to properly.'

I tried not so show how disappointed I was, but Hepzibah reached out an arm around my shoulders. 'Nor did we,' she said.

'Didn't he stay with you? I thought...'

'No. He stayed with the Chief Elder.'

'The Chief Elder!'

'Oh yes. He's much too grand for us now. He'd rather have Mrs Chief Elder fussing around him.'

We looked at each other. Despite our misery we both grinned at the thought of Fin having to be polite to the woman he'd mocked and imitated all his life. Then Hepzibah sighed. 'I hoped he might have talked to you. He seems to have changed so much. He didn't seem to want to talk to us at all. He's not my little brother any more. He's a totally different person. I don't know him now.'

I nodded, dumbly.

'I'm sorry, Amity. I thought...' Her children pulled at her skirts, her husband called to her. 'I don't know what's happened to him. I'm so sorry Amity.' She disappeared with her family.

Despite the clearness of the night, I felt as gloomy and downcast as though the oily black clouds were pressing down harder than ever.

Listen. '*We never wore headscarves — well only a few did. Most of us were proud of our hair, making it look as good as possible, showing it off. We'd spend hours washing it, styling it so it looked its best. When I was about fifteen I dyed my hair pink and purple. My mother was horrified but my father just laughed. One or two women on the island started wearing headscarves when they became religious. The Elders encouraged it until it was compulsory, as if beautiful shiny hair was something to be ashamed off. I never wore a headscarf — unless I was cleaning out the pigs. It's a new custom invented by the Elders.*'

Chapter 15

Shells

The ledge was empty. The food had gone. I'd left it there the day before and now not a crumb of oatcake, flake of cheese or apple pip was left. In its place was a small heap of shells, arranged in pretty fashion, like a thank you. It made me smile.

I looked around, called quietly but no one came. There were a few scuffed marks that could have been footprints in the high dry sand but the tide on the turn had washed anything else away. There was no sound, no gleam of gold. The only sign of life was a cormorant perched on a rock, its wings outstretched. It wasn't going to tell me anything.

Cautiously I left today's supplies, more oatcakes and a piece of ham cut from the side hanging from the kitchen rafters when no one was looking – very difficult in our house. I didn't know why I was leaving the food. I didn't even know who I was leaving it for. I didn't even know if I should be leaving it at all. But in between work at home and in the village, I felt I had to come down and see.

We hadn't heard any gunfire for two days now, but you could feel the fear of it pressing down on us all. Maybe whoever was hiding on the shore was one of the White Star men who was prepared to kill us all for our oil. But I didn't think I was feeding the enemy. I remembered that glimpse of golden gleaming hair and suspected it might be the angel stranger. And he was a peace envoy, the traders said, one that the Sharers, like Father, would want to deal with. Of course I knew that Fin had spirited him away but I never knew where Fin had taken him or what had happened or whether he still needed help. Maybe he was one of the Outlanders trying to persuade The Elders to share our power, the electricity, oil we still had. The Elders, of course, were having none of that.

That had made Father so angry. He'd always been considered a rebel. 'If this power is really a gift from God, then surely we should be sharing it with everyone?' he said, as stamped in from a meeting to organise the security patrols. 'It's not ours to hoard selfishly. We should be rebuilding the world together not fighting among ourselves. Did we learn nothing from the oil wars?'

'Hush, hush,' Mother frowned her disapproval, flapping her apron at him as though she were trying to put out flames. 'That's dangerous godless talk.' She looked frightened. 'That's the sort of talk Shenavar used and look what happened to her.'

'The old woman spoke sense,' said Father. 'She knows the world and has more idea of honesty and justice than some of those Elders who just want to grasp everything for themselves!'

'No, no,' said Mother, 'We have seen the light and we have the oil because we walk in God's way, renouncing the sins of the world.'

Father sighed. He knew he could never make her understand. To make it worse, he'd been one of the handful of men chosen to lead patrols and given a rifle and ammunition. 'I was going to hand it back but then thought it would better if I had it then give it to someone who would be happy to use it at the first provocation. It would take a lot before I could use it against a fellow human being. Lord knows, there are a few enough of us left in this world. Doesn't the Bible say "Thou shalt not kill"?

'The Elders pick and choose their quotations to please themselves,' he went on. Then he saw how panicked Mother was getting, so he sat down by the fire and pulled little Erin onto his knee. 'I hope you'll have a happier country to live in, Erin,' he said and she giggled which made Father smile and Mother relax a little. Just a little.

Many more people were beginning to think like Father. But the Elders shouted everyone down. When they said they had God on their side, it was hard to argue. So we were told to guard the riches we'd been given, be extra godly, extra virtuous. We should walk the narrow path of virtue and duty if we were to enjoy God's bounty. As for me I refused to believe the angel was wicked and if he was hiding on the shoreline then he needed help. And I was the only one who could do it.

I picked up the shells I found arranged on the ledge, turned them over in my hand and almost put them in my pocket. But I wasn't going to get caught like that again. I'd had enough of carrying meaningless tokens close to me all day, so I just threw them back down on the sand.

Then I hurried back home. When I got near our house Callum appeared again and started to walk beside me. Why did he always suddenly appear? 'Have you finished work already?' I demanded.

'Just about,' he said, showing his awful teeth in a grin. 'I thought we could walk home together.'

'Why?' I asked in a tone that made it clear I thought it was the stupidest idea in the world.

He shrugged. I got out my knitting and clicked away, not looking at him once until we got to our house.

Had he been waiting for me, watching? The thought made my skin creep.

Listen. *'Some people turned to religion after the great flood. You couldn't blame them, I suppose. It gave them hope and the courage to carry on. I was glad they took comfort from it. Didn't know, of course, how it was going to end up…'*

Chapter 16

Violins and Mirrors

Mother smashed Father's violin. Deliberately. As I watched, she took it from its hiding place in the box in the weaving shed and threw it onto the floor and stamped on it in the heavy clogs she wore for farm work. 'There! And there!' Her face was screwed up fury as she smashed it as though it were a cockroach. 'That will stop the Devil's music!' She stopped, panting and breathless and gazed at what remained. The violin lay on the stone flags its back broken, splinters of wood all around, its sad silent strings curling in the air.

Father came in before she'd had a chance to clear it up. His face went a ghastly white. Slowly he bent down and picked up the piece, every single one, including the tiniest bits of splinter. He turned over each piece in his hands, stroking them as if they were a living thing, as if he could coax the music back into its broken pieces. 'So it's come to this,' he said. 'This is what our God wants.' He tried for a moment to put the pieces back together, although anyone could see it was hopeless. Then he threw them onto the fire. The smell of burning glue and varnish and horsehair filled the room.

'We have to make ourselves more worthy of God,' said Mother, nervous now, as the little ones clung to her skirts, frightened of what was happening. 'We must not let our hearts and minds be distracted by the world's fripperies. We must concentrate on the word of God.'

Father said nothing. Mother went on. 'These are dangerous times. You shouldn't have that fiddle in the house. You should have destroyed it long ago when the Elders told us. We must...'

'Ay,' said Father. 'I know what they say we must do.'

It was years since Father had played his violin, well, since we'd heard him play it at least, not since the Elders banned music as frivolous and dangerous. They said it whips up emotions that can't always be controlled. Down on the shoreline there'd been a great big bonfire of fiddles and flutes. Trumpets and cornets and even a piano had all gone up in flames and a cloud of thick black smoke. I was young then and turned away, choking. I'd seen the elders watching the flames, their faces flickering shadows in the firelight. Even so, they couldn't hide the glee in their eyes as they watched the death of music.

But Father had hidden his violin. Maybe when we were all out he took it out of its hiding place and played it but I never heard him play again. Yet I remember when I was small Father playing a lively tune while Davy and Fin and Bekah and I danced barefoot around the kitchen. Shenavar was still well then and had clapped and laughed along. Mother hadn't joined in but she hadn't stopped us. I can remember even now Fin taking my hands and whirling me round and round.

The Elders had banned dancing too, of course. Much too dangerous.

'They might have a point there,' Shenavar had laughed with her eyes twinkling. 'There's many a baby come into the world when a lad's taken a lass home after the Friday night dance…'

She said there was music in church once. She said that music was joyful. I can't imagine that. She always used to sing around the house, when she was working in the kitchen or playing with the children. She used to sing to me, hymns sometimes and all sorts of other songs about boys and girls and love and hope. We never had hymns in our church. But Shenavar said her world had been full of music. You could carry it with you, and listen while you worked or walked or travelled, she said, all sorts of music, whatever you wanted. Thousands upon thousands of tunes and songs that she could listen to on her phone. But I didn't know how that worked. She said there was bound to be music in Outland because it was part of human nature, that it nourished the soul. Music had power. Music and dancing sounded fun. That's why it wasn't allowed.

'Do you remember the dancing?' I asked Bekah as we struggled with the big baskets of our family washing in the communal laundry.

'Shh!' said Bekah looking anxiously around her at the other women filling machines or sorting clothes and Priscilla' sly eyes watching us. Then she came closer to me and almost whispered. 'Of course I do, me and Davy, you and Fin in your kitchen with your Father playing the fiddle. Ah, but we were only bairns then, wouldn't it be grand to be doing that again?' Her eyes became dreamy. 'Imagine holding hands with Davy, twirling around while the music played. I think of it sometimes. For years I've tried to remember the tune in my head.'

'I know it,' I said. 'Sometimes when Father's not thinking or he thinks no-one's listening he sings it to himself.' Quietly I started to hum the jolly, jigging dance tune.

'That's it!' said Bekah and joined in, quietly at first but then getting a bit carried away.

Then one of the old ladies near us carefully folding an endless pile of work-shirts laughed, 'Eeh, I remember that!' she said and started singing too, loudly clearly, the old song. Her eyes lit up and she smiled broadly as she abandoned the shirts, pulled up her heavy skirt until it was above her ankles and tried a few tentative dance steps past the washing machines.

More of the women joined in until there was quite a crowd dancing and singing in the steamy, soapy warmth of the laundry and the atmosphere buzzed with light hearted happiness. From the corner of my eye I could see Priscilla slipping out of the door.

Bekah and I looked at each other and laughed. What had we started? But we shrugged our shoulders and followed the older women's steps and jigged up and down until we were breathless. Then a door banged open.

A hand slammed down on top of one of the machines and voice boomed out. 'What on earth is going on here? Has the Devil got into you all?' Mrs Chief Elder. Her face was as sour as week old milk and her voice like a corncrake, echoing around the big stone-flagged room. 'Have you no sense of what is fitting?' she snapped, while Priscilla stood just behind her, smiling smugly. 'Were you singing and....' her face screwed up in agonies as if she could barely get the word out until finally she almos spat '...*dancing?*'

'Just a moment's weakness, ma'am,' said one of the old ladies. 'We are but weak creatures of clay. It won't happen again.'

'It had better not,' boomed Mrs Chief Elder.

We all got quietly and purposefully on with doing our washing. But as I loaded up the basket the jigging tune still danced through my head and almost into my toes.

That evening Mother took the mirror from my bedroom.

'Oh no!' I cried as she took it down. The mirror came from Australia which was the other side of the world. Shenavar had brought it back when she'd visited her sister there before the wars. She never knew what had become of her sister. Because no one could travel through the stinking fires that circled the middle of the globe, we weren't even sure if Australia was still there.

'Shenavar gave me that!' I said to Mother.

'And that's even more reason to take it away,' said Mother. 'That woman has always had too much influence in this house, even when she's long been as good as dead. It's time for new ways. Anyway, you spend too much time gazing at it. You'll see the Devil in that mirror one day if I don't stop you!'

'But it's the only mirror in the house!'

'There's one by the back door.'

'But that's tiny and blotchy and mottled and you can't see in it.'

'You can see well enough to know if your headscarf is on straight and that's all that matters.'

'But I loved Shenavar's mirror!' It had a pretty frame of blue and white flowers and sometimes I would look in it practising different styles for my hair - which I'd never be able to use - or seeing if my lips were pink or if the sun had given me freckles. Bekah and Lowri had concocted a lotion to whiten our freckles but it was all very secret. The Elders would whip us if they thought we were guilty of vanity.

'Mother!' I pleaded

'It behoves us to concentrate our minds on God in these difficult times,' she said 'We must become more godly and renounce our frivolous ways.'

So the mirror went. After Father had said not a word about his violin, I felt I couldn't make a fuss about a mirror.

Listen. '*My first job was in a coffee shop on Saturday mornings. With my wages I bought a pair of purple shoes with narrow straps and heels so high and thin I could hardly walk in them. My mother laughed and said they were ridiculous but it was my money and I could do what I liked with it.*'

Chapter 17

A Voice from the Past

The noise was so strange, so unexpected. It seemed to come from so far away that at first I thought it was a small breeze rattling the dry husks of barley. I stopped my work to listen. Then with a shock, I realised that Shenavar had spoken.

'Dwr,' she said, which in our language meant water. Her voice was so dry and brittle and barely had the strength to get out into the air. Then she said the same word in English 'water.'

I'd been putting clean sheets on her bed, telling her about the day before when I'd taken more food down to the cave and found three feathers arranged on the ledge. 'It must be a thank you, mustn't it?' I prattled on until I heard the tiny noise and stopped. She raised a hand a fraction as I stood still holding the coverlet. She was so tiny, slumped sideways in her chair. She said again 'Dwr' her voice, still faint and blurred.

I dropped the coverlet and rushed to pour her a glass of water and supported her tiny body as she drank it. 'Water' she said in English. Then slowly, and so quietly I could hardly hear, with many pauses, 'I would ..I should… have taught… you English.'

The words came slowly on tiny scratchy puffs of breath. But her eyes were bright and full of life. I knelt beside her.

'Your medicine Shenavar!' I said. It was days now since she'd had her medicine.

'Too late,' she said. 'There' s not .. long now. It … fogged …my brain. That's what… they wanted. They don't like… people …to argue.'

'Who doesn't? The Elders you mean?' I asked. 'You mean the medicine made you ill?'

'Made…me….sleep so much. Couldn't…think,' she whispered.

'But that's wicked!' I said. 'You were the only one who ever stood up to them!'

Shenavar's mouth puckered into a half smile. 'Too late now,' she said, every word gasped with the effort as if she were pushing a boulder up hill.

I was stroking her hand, so thin and frail that I could see every bone through the skin. There was a long pause and I thought she'd gone back to sleep. But no, she was clearly summoning up her strength as she whispered. 'You must …give him the … box. Your … angel. He must have… the box.'

Now I knew she'd been listening to all I'd said for the past weeks. Shocked and excited, 'The *sat.com* box?' I said.

She nodded.

'But what is it? Why is the box so important?'

She gave the smallest, feeblest wave of her hand. 'I

should never.. have brought you here,' she whispered. 'But it seemed ..best…back then.' Then her eyes closed, her chin slumped and I knew this time that she really had lapsed back to sleep.

What did she mean - she should never have brought me here? I knew I wasn't born into this family but knew no more than that. I was about ten when I started asking about my original family. But Mother just said 'Didn't we take you in when you had nobody? So it behoves you to be a dutiful daughter.' And I tried to be that dutiful daughter, I really tried. But sometimes it was just so hard.

And the box! Shenavar obviously knew what the box was. She knew it must belong to the stranger. I would have to get it to him. Shenavar had spoken for the first time for years. How could I ignore what she said?

That afternoon I was meant to be doing my turn in the polytunnels, potting up young plants. Instead, I went straight down to the otter beach. The boat was still there, well-hidden between the rocks. But there was no sign of a human being. There were two razor clam shells there as a thank you today. I left a few oatcakes and cheese on the ledge and looked around. There were marks above the waterline in the soft powdery sand. They were too indistinct to make out properly but they were a stride apart and led to the cave. I tiptoed inside. Here, where the tide hadn't reached but the sand was firmer, there were scuffed footprints and marks. Someone had been sitting, stretched out, leaning against the rock wall.

'Hello?' I called softly. No reply.

At the very back of the cave I carefully moved the heap of pebbles and uncovered the *sat.com* box. Then I brought it nearer the entrance and placed it on a ledge near the food. The angel - if it was the angel - would see it straightaway but it was still unlikely that anyone else would find it. If they did, they wouldn't know what to do with it, any more than I did. 'Thank you Shenavar for telling me what to do,' I thought, as I made sure the box was safe. I wish I knew why it was so important. Maybe she'd tell me tomorrow.

Now she could speak again, even if only so slowly and painfully, there were so many things I wanted to ask her, so many questions. Starting with where she'd brought me from. And the stories that the trader man Xander had hinted at. And more stories! So much to know about the world now I was older and knew what to ask.

I looked around the cave trying to find some more signs of the angel. But there was nothing. I waited for a while. Then I realised that I'd been there too long. People would be missing me. I had to go. Besides, I couldn't wait to talk to Shenavar again. I had so much to ask her! I clambered back over the rocks and along the stepping stones as quickly as I could and almost ran up the path to the village.

Of course, Callum was in the track by the polytunnels, watching out for me. I tried to dodge him, but he'd seen me. I tried to walk straight past him. But this time he looked different. As if he was trying to be nice. Scary. He grabbed my hand. 'Get off, Callum!' I tried to pull away from him but he turned me round so I had to stop and look at him.

'Shenavar died this afternoon,' he blurted out. 'Sorry, Amity. Elspeth went to the polytunnels after school to tell you. But they said you weren't there. You hadn't been there all afternoon.' He had a sly air of triumph as he said this but I was too shocked to care.

'Shenavar can't be dead!' I cried. 'This morning she was better than she's been for years. She even...'

'She even what?' asked Callum, his hand still gripping mine as he stood too close to me with his stinky onion breath.

'She even looked like she was trying to say something,' I said. I wasn't going to tell him that she actually had spoken. And certainly not what she'd said.

'Huh! The old lady hasn't spoken for years and when she did it was only to cause trouble.' Callum sneered. 'Best thing for her, this. She's been virtually dead for years. If she'd been a dog we'd have put her out of her misery years ago. If...'

'Shut up! Just shut UP!' I shouted. 'How *dare* you say such things about her?' He moved even closer, tried to grab my other hand too, but I pulled free and pushed him out of my way, so he stumbled back and nearly fell. I heard him shouting behind me as I raced home, dreading what I'd find there.

Listen. *'It had been another long winter. We'd lost so many men but we had more children to care for. We were exhausted. Then one day we saw a boat! We ran down to cliffs and guided it round to where the rocks were least dangerous but it couldn't get into shore and turned away. The men in it shouted to us but the wind whipped away their words as we watched them go. That was a bad night.*

'It was six weeks before they came back again and managed to land. They couldn't believe we had survived so long and had so many healthy children. They were men who had been working in the oil refineries or in the navy base and were very disciplined and decent. And some from the old religious centre a few miles inland. They brought us flour and meat and above all news of other people. We felt we had rejoined the world.'

111

Chapter 18

The Truth

'**I**'ve come for the sake of the old lady. She was a fine woman and a grand teacher,' said Bekah's grandfather. 'The last of her kind and a brave, wise woman.' He was one of the few who came to Shenavar's funeral. People were kind enough and stopped us in the street and said 'I'm sorry for your loss.' But they were too scared to come to the church because they knew the Elders disapproved of Shenavar.

'But if it wasn't for her,' went on Bekah's grandfather, 'I don't think any of us would be here. No one on the Island would have survived. Shenavar was only little but, by, she was tough. She made people do what was right. Right from when I was a little lad I remember my parents saying that. They were alongside her, through the wars and afterwards. Saved them all, she did, they said.'

Some of the island men, not old enough to remember the oil wars and the years immediately afterwards, came to the funeral for Father's sake. They came because they, too, believed in her notion of sharing what resources we had with Outland.

'There's been enough wars,' said one old man quietly as he shook Father's hand. 'The old lady talked sense. There's barely a handful of us left so what stupidity is to kill each other? What then will become of the world?'

Mother, who was wearing her hat, glared at him to be quiet as the elders drew near. The elders conducted the funeral as briskly as possible. The Chief Elder - who normally loved the sound of his own voice and could keep a funeral eulogy going for an hour or more - glossed over all she'd done for the island in the wars and beyond and talked for no more than five minutes. 'She did much to help the community and was a much respected teacher,' was about all he said. Hateful man! Couldn't even be generous to her when she was dead.

'Nothing about the way she helped the island survive in the war,' I muttered to Lowri. 'Or about the Hunger Years. She practically saved this island! Nothing about her campaigns for co-operation with Outland. Nothing about the way she fought for the God she had grown up with, nothing about how she had condemned the Elders as petty-minded kill joys.'

'Well, you could hardly expect them to say that, could you?' asked Lowri reasonably.

But I wasn't feeling reasonable. If you hadn't known anything about Shenavar you wouldn't have been any the wiser after the Elder's short speech. I wanted to stand up and tell everyone of the stories she told, of how she made me realise that there was a world out there full of ideas so much bigger than what the Elders tried to tell us. That books are riches to be enjoyed not something to be feared. That is was no sin to sing or dance and be happy. That we should be reaching out to the world, not keeping everything to ourselves like a dog with a bone, snarling at anyone who dares to come near. Shenavar was only little but her ideas were as big as the world, the universe, itself.

We walked in our small procession - just the family and the Elders struggling against the wind up the hill to the graveyard, where Father and Bryn had dug the grave the day before. The wind swirled with the scent of fresh wet earth and torn grass before it snatched it away again. The sky was dark and the wind whistled through the cracks between the stones of the graveyard wall and roared over the hill down to the sea. Mother hung onto her hat and I wrapped my King's Academy blazer tight around me and feared I would be almost blown away.

The men lowered the tiny coffin into the grave and committed Shenavar's soul to the Lord. As we threw the handfuls of earth onto coffin, one of the Elders said 'Ah, but she's gone to a better place. Now she can rest in peace.' Despite the swirling wind and the sadness of the occasion, he looked … relieved.

That's it, he looked *relieved* and pleased. It was that look that made me angry. So angry that my patience snapped. 'You mean *you* can rest in peace!' I shouted, the crumbs of the grave's stony soil still clinging to my frozen fingers. 'The only person who challenged you is out of the way now!' Once I started, I couldn't stop. 'Now you don't have to drug her any more! Coming to the house every month, praying over her, making out you were being so good and godly bringing her special drugs for the pain. No you weren't! You were gagging her, keeping her silent so she wouldn't be able to speak out and tell you how wicked you really are!' I took a breath. 'You sentenced her to a living death because she was the only one who dared speak out against you. You… Arrggh!'

Mother had slapped me, hard. The wind gave extra strength to her hand and I felt my face burn and my teeth judder. I staggered back and fell against the freshly-dug earth and back nearly into the grave on top of the coffin. Lowri and Elspeth and Bryn and Iolo and the rest of them were looking at me horrified. The Elders looked like a row of angry black crows, their heads bobbing in fury.

But I wasn't going to stop now. I stood upright, plunging my hand into the cold damp heap of soil and stones beside the grave, and shouted at the Elders, my voice howling into the wind. 'She told me before she died. You drugged her! She said! Those medicines you brought her. They weren't to make her better, they were to keep her quiet! Because she talked sense and you didn't want people to hear!' I took another deep breath. 'You pretend to be so good but you are wicked, wicked men!'

Father came up to me and wrapped his arms tightly round me, pinning my arms to my side and holding my head firmly close to him so I could smell the smoky tweed of his jacket and could hardly breathe. 'Shush child!' he said. 'Shush. This isn't the time nor place.' Through the muffle of Father's jacket I could hear the Elders booming about 'False witness!' and 'Blasphemy! and 'Wickedness, wickedness.' And the sound of earth on the coffin as Iolo and Bryn hurriedly filled in the grave.

Mother crying and saying 'I'm sorry, she's sorry. She didn't mean it. She was so close to the old lady. Forgive her. She didn't mean it.'

'But I did!' I tried to say, but Father held my head closer to his chest so the words were muffled. I tried to wriggle free but he had me tight.

Then from the corner of my eye I could see the sky over the sea suddenly light up. We all stiffened in fear that it was gunfire. Then there was a crack of thunder and another flash. 'Lightning!' said Lowri. 'Going into the sea.' And the first heavy drops of rain.

'Ah, trust the old lady not to go quietly,' said one of the old men.

We all dashed down the hill again. Father and Mother holding tightly on to each of my arms, so I kept stumbling – and dragging me back to my feet when I did. Mother apologising all the time to the Elders and Father and the Elders looking grim-faced.

Well, I'd done it now.

Back home Father pulled me into the privacy of Shenavar's room. My face and teeth still ached from Mother's slap.

He turned me to face him. 'Was it true what you said, child?' he asked

I nodded and told him of that last morning, of Shenavar's whispery voice as dry as a husk. I told him everything she said - about the Elders and the medicine. He nodded when I said that. Perhaps he'd already suspected something of the sort. Then I told him what she said about wanting to teach me English. But I didn't tell him about the angel and the *sat. com* box. Not about that. 'She said she should never have brought me here. What did she mean by that?'

'I don't know,' said Father. 'It was she who brought you to our door when you were a little toddling child.'

'But where did I come from?'

'I don't know. I just thought you were from the other side of the island. She never said otherwise and we just assumed... Shenavar knew everyone and everybody, who needed help, who could cope and who couldn't. It was a difficult time. Not as bad as the hungry years by all accounts but there'd been illness and accidents. So many babies without parents and parents without babies. It was hard to keep track.

'Just when we'd got our community going and had some hope for the future there'd been a winter of great illness and many people had died. People were taking care of whoever they could. It was a confused time. And that was the time the Traders came, the first time for a year, the time we had so much work to do repairing the wind turbines...'

'You mean I came here at the same time as the traders?'

'Well I suppose so, yes.'

'Could I have come with the traders?' That would explain the way Xander thought I knew of Sheanavar's adventures. Was it too much of a coincidence that I had arrived at just that time?

Father looked baffled. 'But why on earth would they do that child? The traders look after their own babies and they wouldn't bring a baby from Outland all the way to here to be cared for, would they?'

No, it didn't seem sensible. And yet...

'Your mother and I had Davy, and Lowri was a new baby. But Shenavar brought you to us and asked us to take you in and we did. She might have told us where you came from but I seem to think she was deliberately vague. I remember thinking that maybe your birth mother had been some foolish girl caught before she had a chance to wed. Your mother feared you might have bad blood. But it's a long time ago and I can't quite recall now.

'And it didn't matter a jot because we loved you straight away. You and Davy used to prattle away to each other. You talked such nonsense! But you were friends from the very beginning. We never thought but that you were one of our own.'

'I know, Father and I thank you for that.'

'You should thank your mother too, child.'

Difficult when my teeth were still rattling around my jaw.

'And did Shenavar say nothing else?' There was an eager light in his eyes.

I shook my head, hating to disappoint him. 'The effort of talking seemed so great. Every word was a struggle for her. And I thought there'd be more time to talk… I didn't know…' Tears welled up in my eyes.

'Ay,' said Father. 'I would have liked to have heard her voice again, liked to have heard what she had to say…' There was a moment's silence. Then he got to his feet. 'But you were foolish to spit it out like that at The Elders. Foolish and impudent – whatever the truth. They will never forgive you.' He looked rueful. 'Neither will your mother. You'd have been far better holding your tongue. You've made your life much harder child and that's something you alone will have to deal with. You were lucky there was no one else around, otherwise I think the Elders would have been up for having you apologise in front of the entire congregation in church. But we will go to the Chief Elder now.'

I gasped. 'No!'

'Yes,' said Father with steel in his voice. 'We will go to the Chief Elder now and you will apologise for your outburst. For the sake of your brothers and sisters and your mother.'

There was no arguing with that. Off we went. Mrs Chief Elder look surprised to see me which meant he hadn't even told her. Interesting. And as I walked into his study I saw a quick look of fear on the Chief Elder's face. Almost immediately replaced by his normal look of stuffed sanctimony.

'My daughter has come to apologise,' said my father.

I curtseyed deeply but held my head high. 'I am sorry sir for my outburst. It was unseemly and ill-judged, especially on such an occasion.' See, I hadn't actually said it wasn't true.

The Chief Elder glared at me. I remembered that brief look of fear. I gazed back, as steadily as I could. Instead of the rant I'd expected and the denunciation and the threats of hellfire, he just prayed over me for five minutes and hoped that I would learn to curb my tongue and learn judgement.

'So,' said Father as we walked back home. 'You and I know the truth, child and the Chief Elder knows that we know. My thinking is that we'll hear no more about it now.' When we got back to the house he handed me a package carefully wrapped in an ancient carrier bag, so old it was brittle and flaking apart. 'Shenavar's notebooks,' he said. 'The Elders took her books but they had no right to these so I wouldn't let them take them. I've kept them for you. I'm not sure they'll be much use to you. And I'm not sure this is the time to give them to you. But here you are.'

'Thank you,' I said taking them carefully and, for

once and without thinking, I curtseyed to Father.

He patted my shoulder. 'You were always good to Shenavar. I'm glad of that,' he said. 'But watch your tongue, child and keep your thoughts to yourself. And have some respect for your mother.'

Father might have been prepared to forgive and forget my outburst in the graveyard but Mother certainly wasn't. After that day she harassed me from morn till night, giving me the worst jobs, hardly allowing me to sit. Every time she looked at me she muttered 'Blasphemer! Sinner!' Her favourite was, 'How sharper than a serpent's tooth to have an ungrateful child.'

She wasted no time clearing out Shenavar's room. Elspeth and Morag were going to have that. I'd already rescued her phone (Why? It was useless but it had been so important to her…) and the New York snow shaker. And I'd taken the guide to London and hidden it under my mattress. Mother kept one or two of the pretty boxes and glasses but the coffee maker she gave to Father in case he could use the plastic casing for something. The empty lipstick she threw on the fire where it eventually twisted out of shape and vanished into the ashes. 'We'll have no thoughts of painted women here!' she said.

'Perhaps not,' said Father. 'But remember Shenavar was a remarkable woman. Without her…'

'Yes, yes, yes,' said Mother, free now that Shenavar was no longer with us, 'I know that Shenevar was wonderful in the war and the Hungry Years. But that was then. Times have changed. If we are to survive we all need to be closer to God. Some of us' - with a fierce look at me - 'have further to go than others.'

The Father said 'If it hadn't been for Shenavar and people like her, none of us would be here today. You'd do well to mind that.'

'I mind what the Elders say!' she retorted. 'And how we can convince them we are a decent God-fearing family when we have such a shameless, wanton daughter. All we've done for her and this is how she repays us!' And she wept into her apron.

'But I only told the truth, Mother!' I said.

'Truth! Truth! What do you know of truth?' Mother came towards me as if she would hit me again. 'The only truth I know now is that we are shamed in front of the Elders, our good name gone. I can barely hold my head up as a respectable woman after nurturing such a viper in my bosom!'

I longed to escape and look at the notebooks but Mother had other ideas. 'The dairy is in a terrible state,' she cried. It wasn't of course. It was always spotless. 'Get in there now and scrub it all, the shelves and the floors. The pans need scalding again. Go!'

As I knelt and scrubbed I worked out my plan. I would get myself ready. When the traders came back again, whether later in the year or not until next spring, I would go with them. The man Xander, whose grandfather had been a friend of Shenavar, I was sure he would take me. He'd brought me here. I felt sure of that now. So it was only right he would take me back. If not, then it would be no hard thing to sneak into a wagon under the tarpaulin. I'd only have to stay hidden until they got across to Mainland and it would be impossible for me to come back. Somehow I would get away from the island. All I need take was my knitting needles and I could maybe pay my way in the outside world.

By the time I finished the dairy it was dark. Everyone was in bed, apart from Mother who had sat up knitting in the firelight to make sure I finished my task. 'I've told Lowri that you will do the milking in the morning,' she said. 'You'll have more time now without the old woman to look after.'

'Yes Mother,' I said dutifully. There was no point in arguing. I hung my damp skirt to dry out over the rack near the fire and made my way upstairs by the light of a stub of candle. I was bone weary and my fingers were raw from the water and soap and scrubbing but still I couldn't wait to read Shenavar's notebooks.

Careful not to waken Lowri, I unwrapped the brittle carrier bag, watching the flakes of it drift onto my blankets. Inside was a big envelope, its creases worn so thin that they were nearly slits. Inside that there were three big notebooks, a smaller, thinner one and some scraps of paper covered in writing. The notebook covers were faded, the edges of the pages had yellowed with age. But inside the writing was as bright as new, tiny, beautifully neat, filling every line with occasional headings that looked like dates.

I brought the candle as close as I dared - I didn't want to drip wax on the precious books - and settled down eagerly to read. But I couldn't. The writing was neat. The ink hardly faded. The letters were clear. But I couldn't read a word. Shenavar had written all her notebooks in English...

Listen. *'At first it worked well. The men had the knowledge to rebuild the turbines. Despite the black clouds we grew more food, raised more animals. We established a proper little society and made rules among ourselves. Some people were very religious. There was no harm in that.*

'Then we had a bad winter and a worse summer as the smoky black clouds hardly lifted at all. The religious men decided we were being punished by God. Nonsense of course. But the idea spread. Frightened people are easy to convince.'

Chapter 19

Confined

We could see the fire storm racing in across the sky. Darkness covered the face of the earth and tiny hot hailstones of tar rained down on us.

'Quick!' yelled Mother 'Get the stock in!'

Lowri ran out to lead the cows into the byre. Elspeth and I shooed the hens into the hen house. They clucked indignantly and fluttered up into the air. I could see tiny hot specks land on their wings and feel them too on my shoulders. Bryn saw to the pig. The little ones rushed round collecting up eggs. Out in the distant darkness I could see Father and Callum and other men and dogs trying to persuade panicking sheep into the lambing sheds.

We had to get as much as possible under cover. When the black storm comes the tar burns into skin and hide and wool. It covers the ground and sinks into the soil, killing things growing there. It burns holes into the roof of the polytunnels. We just about managed to get back in the house before everything went dark and the men too ran for cover.

'Ah I thought we'd seen the last of these!' said Father as he and Callum stamped into the kitchen. Their caps were covered with a shiny, tarry sheen. There were yet more holes in his ancient waterproof and their boots left oily prints on the floor. Apart from seeing to the animals, we stayed indoors while the blackness raged over us. The smell of the oil seeped through the gaps in the doors and windows and into the house. It was on our clothes, on our skin. It was in the milk we drank and the food we ate. It mingled with the smell of peat from the fire and too many people. We longed for fresh air.

It was dark for days.

'It's God's punishment for our sins, a warning to bring us back to the ways of righteousness,' wailed Mother, twisting her apron over and over again in her anxious, worried hands. 'And you, girl! You made it worse by speaking so to the Elders. Oh,' she wailed, covering her face, 'Look what you've done! I can't believe it from one I have nurtured as my own.'

'It wasn't me who made the weather!' I cried. (I didn't, did I? Was that the way God works?) 'It was the Elders!' I said. 'They did wrong, trying to keep Shenavar quiet.'

'Whatever they did, they did for God's purpose,' she snapped back. 'Not out of wickedness and blasphemy like you, girl!'

She was so angry with me that I almost began to believe her. But then I remembered all I'd done was tell the truth. How could that be a sin?

The animals were restless and unhappy. We could hear their plaintive cries and could do little apart from keep them fed and watered. The only time we got out was to grope our way through the choking cloud to go to church, scarves and shawls over our mouths to stop us breathing in the tar. There were prayer meetings every day. But the very young and the very old didn't go. They were excused because the cloud could have killed them.

Otherwise we were all trapped indoors, including Nutmeg, who was the only one who was happy about the black cloud. It meant instead of having to sleep in the barn, he could come into the house and stretch out on the rug in front of the fire. He liked to lie on people's feet and it was very comforting to feel his doggy warmth across us.

We had one wind-up lamp. Sometimes Mother sat with it on her lap, winding, winding, winding as if she could single-handedly keep the darkness away for ever. Otherwise we got on with our lives by candlelight and the light of the fire, carding, spinning, knitting, sewing, preparing what food we could. Father and the boys mended shoes and tools or sometimes Father would escape to his weaving shed. The rhythm of the shuttle soothed him. And it got him away from the noise of the house, even though Lowri and I tried to keep the little ones from getting too fretful.

One afternoon Iolo and Erin were playing with the Noah's Ark that had been Father's once years ago and his father's before that. The little wooden figures were long faded and bashed about. Their features had been smoothed into roundness and one or two of the figures had lost their mate. So the zebra was always paired with a monkey and the snake slithered into the ark suspiciously alone. Erin was lining up the animals in pairs and Iolo was making them go up the ramp two by two. 'Moo!' said Iolo as he moved the lions up the ramp.

'Lions don't go moo!' I said, trying to stop baby Liam from eating the little wooden hens.

'Then how do they go?' asked Iolo, reasonably enough.

'I don't know,' I said helplessly. 'I've never seen a lion or heard one. Or a giraffe. Or a leopard. Or an elephant, a zebra, a monkey or a rhino. I've never seen *any* of those creatures. Or even know anyone who has. I don't know if they really look like that. I don't know if they're really called that. We might have got the names all wrong. We might be calling the elephant a zebra or the rhino a giraffe. I don't know. And I've no idea at all what sound they make.'

Would I ever see anything that wasn't on our island? Was all I'd ever see in this world was what I'd already seen? Maybe there was nothing new for me. We didn't even have pictures of animals to look at. Nothing. I shuddered.

'The psalmist says,' said Father sensing what I was thinking, 'that "the young lions roar for their prey". But they are only cats really, aren't they? And I don't know how big they are. So maybe they make a noise like a cat. A sort of very loud meow only bigger. Or a purr loud enough to wake you. Maybe that's a roaring noise. Or spit when they're angry. I don't know.' He shrugged

'What about giraffes?' I asked, picking up the faded, battered little giraffe. 'And elephants and zebras?' How do we know what they sounded like? Or how big they are? Or if they really exist at all?'

Father shrugged again. 'I don't know. I don't know if anyone does. And I don't suppose we'll ever see one to find out.'

127

'But there are so many things we'll never see!' I raised my voice. 'And so many things we'll never know!'

Father looked angry. 'Hush child!' he said. 'And if you can't amuse the little ones without getting into a temper, then you'd better take yourself off and find some work to do.'

I got to my feet and stomped off to find Lowri in the little room next to the dairy, where she was making one of her potions.

'Amity, why do you have to ask so many questions when you know they only make people angry? Here…' She passed me a pestle and a mortar full of broken twigs. '..crush these for me until they're as fine as you can make them, like powder, like dust.'

I took them and started pushing and grinding with the pestle. It was hard work and made my shoulder ache. But it was something to do. I could smell him before I saw him. Even from feet away, that faint sour smell of sweaty, unwashed skin and uncleaned teeth.

'Callum,' I said, without even turning round. 'Do you have to stand there? Haven't you got anything better to do?'

'Not just now. Anyway, I can stand here if I like. It's as much my house as yours.'

I was about to snap that he was only a lodger. But he was right. I'd lived there longer than him but he at least was blood kin to Mother, while I was nothing, no kin at all. I had less right in this home and family than the awful Callum. I was just the cuckoo in this crowded nest. That wasn't a comfortable feeling.

The twigs were already turning to a lumpy sort of splintery ooze. I pressed harder on the pestle, twisting it round, pretending it was Callum's leering face and then I tried to put Callum out of my mind, not even dignify him with a space in my head or my thoughts.

Instead, even though I knew it was all over for Fin and me I still wondered where he was, what he was doing… And I wondered about the angel in the cave at otter rocks and how he was managing in the great blackness.

Without Shenavar's room I had nowhere to escape to, nowhere to read my book. I tried to teach the little ones their letters, writing them on a slate. Iolo spelled everything out laboriously and stumbled over the letters.

Erin came toddling up, took one look and read the words right off. She'd been listening when I'd tried to teach Iolo and had soaked it all up into her tiny head.

'Clever girl!' said Father. 'Only two and already you know your letters!'

Mother sniffed disapprovingly. 'At least she won't have Shenavar to fill her head with ideas and make her think she's as good as a boy.'

'Mother!' I was about to defend Shenavar's memory and say that Erin was obviously quicker than Iolo though he was two years older but Father intervened. 'Hush now hush. We've clever sons and clever daughters and we're all too closed in together now to quarrel.' He gave me a look which made me bite my lip and hold my tongue even though I had much else I could have said. I knew I'd said too much at the graveside. But I didn't care that the Elders knew what I knew. I hope it made them suffer!

So we all sat together imprisoned indoors in the darkness.

But without work to do outside, even with all the jobs Mother kept finding for me, I had more chance to study Shenavar's notebooks. I'd puzzled for hours over them and their careful English entries.

But Shenavar had left me a clue. The smaller thinner book in the bag wasn't a diary or an ordinary notebook. It took me a while to see what it was and then I realised that Shenavar had started to write a book on teaching English. She was proud of our Celtic language but must have realised that English would be useful. There wasn't much of it and it was very simple. Much like Iolo's reading book. There were pictures and underneath in English 'dog', 'cat.' But there was a long list of words in the back in both English and Celtic so you could translate between them.

In our bedroom, by candlelight - I didn't dare risk Mother's anger by looking at the books in her sight - Lowri and I had quietly practised the words. 'Dog' we said, not knowing if we were saying properly. 'Cat.' 'How do you know that's the right way to say it?' asked Lowri, trying to get her tongue around 'Big dog. Small cat.'

'I don't.' I said. 'But it sort of sounds right, somehow.'

We kept trying. 'Hello. My name is Amity.'

'Hello. My name is Lowri.'

'The dog is big.'

'The cat is small.'

'If we ever meet anyone from Outland it's not going to get us very far, is it?' laughed Lowri. 'Once we've talked about their dog and their cat, that's going to be it.'

'We have to keep trying!' I said but then it struck me as silly too and we both got the giggles and were rolling round the bed laughing so much until we got the hiccups and thought we would choke until Mother shouted up for to stop being silly and come downstairs and make ourselves useful.

Listen. '*Before the war I always wore nail polish. All colours from pink and purple to blue, green and black. Lovely tiny bottles, in a row on the shelf. After we became an island we had so much hard work to do that my hands were rough and red, my nails cracked and ragged. But one day in the ruins of a house I found a bottle of dark red polish. There was just enough for me and my friend Lola to do our nails. Just the smell when we unscrewed the lid and took the little brush out was enough to take us back to who we used to be. Ridiculous really but it made us very happy for a while.*'

Chapter 20

The Book

'**G**ive it back to me! Give it *back!*'

I leaped up but Callum, taunting, gloating was holding the precious piece of paper just out of my reach. It was a page from my book about London. One with the bridge that looked like a castle and went up and down to let the ships through. He must have found my book and ripped the page out - ripped it out! Now his dirty yellow teeth were bared in a grin as he passed the piece of paper from hand to hand above his head and way above mine.

In fury I thumped my fists against his chest, but that just made him laugh the more. As I pounded him in my anger I could hear his mocking laugh above me and smell the stench of him, so foul I could barely breathe.

The day before, desperate to get away from the crowded, stifling, squabbling house, I'd gone through the blackness to check on the hens and then the sheep in the barn. I'd smuggled my book under my apron and had a few minutes blissful peace huddled up in the dim light on the narrow platform that was the hay loft. Below me was the squawk and smell of too many animals crowded in to too small a space. Outside the black clouds swirled in the rising wind but for a while I gazed at my book and was transported to a city of parks and gardens and sunshine and elegant buildings. Then I heard footsteps striding down from the house, the rattle of the barn door opening and there were Bryn and Callum pushing their way through the noisy sheep.

'What are you doing here?' demanded Callum, smacking an old ewe on her rump to get her to move out of his way.

'Looking for eggs,' I said as I stuffed the book under the corner of a sack. 'But I've only found two. The hens are really off laying at the moment.' I was blushing, I knew, and making too much fuss about pretending to search the hay for the eggs I'd found earlier.

'You might have fed the sheep and saved us the bother,' grumbled Bryn, while Callum just stared at me.

I clambered down the ladder, holding on with one hand as I carefully carried the eggs in the other. Then I pushed my way through the noisy sheep, out into the blackness and into the house. I'd have to find an excuse to go back as soon as possible and rescue my book. I didn't get the chance.

Now I was just in the kitchen feeding Liam when Callum came stamping in from the barn. He took his boots off and then came over to me with gloating smile. 'Look what I've got...' he chanted, waving a piece of paper in front of me.

Straightaway I'd recognised what it was.

133

'You've ripped it!' I said, horrified that he could have damaged something so precious. 'How could you?' Now he was mocking me, teasing and my head was filled with the stink of him. My anger boiled over. With the strength of pure anger, I flew up at his face, his horrid slimy, grimy grinning face and I thumped and clawed him and scratched him and leapt up and did it again. I'd caught him by surprise. He dropped the page as he put his hands in front of his face to protect it from me.

'You wild cat!' he spat at me. 'You dirty little wild cat.'

He reached out to grab me but I was too quick for him. I snatched the page off the floor and dodged out of his way.

'What's going on in there?' shouted Mother from the next room. If she knew I still had a book she would throw it on the fire.

'Just Callum being stupid,' I muttered as I rushed through and up to my bedroom.

I smoothed the page carefully and laid it under the mattress to get the creases out. Later I crept out to the barn and rescued the book where Callum had left it lying. Father or Bryn could easily have seen it. I tucked the page back in and waited for Callum to tell my parents about the book.

But strangely, he didn't. When Father said 'Good grief, boy, what have you done to your face?' he even muttered something about one of the metal rakes falling on him when he tripped over a sheep.

For a moment I thought I'd had a reprieve. Then I saw him looking at me across the room. There was such a look in his eyes that I realised that he knew the longer I waited for him to say about the book, the more I would suffer.

I hated him.

Listen. *'We found small patches of fertile ground in sheltered spots where the worst of the smoke hadn't penetrated. We planted those with the few seeds we had. When the land fell into the sea we were able to dig into the sides for clean soil and carried it to the old hotel where they had a big conservatory. They used to have weddings and dances there but we turned it into a greenhouse.'*

Chapter 21

After the storm

At last, after days of darkness, the black cloud passed, blown away by wild storms, howling winds and torrential rains. The windows rattled. Rain poured down the chimney and put out the fires. One of the wind turbines crashed, thundering to the earth. Sheets from the polytunnels billowed past us, bits of fence all went racing past making a mighty roar.

Only Callum and Father went to see to the animals. They were the only ones who could stand up outside. The rest of us would have been blown away. Lowri spent some time with her plants and herbs but sighed with frustration because she needed something she didn't have or couldn't get. Elspeth helped her sometimes. Though only very young, she too already seemed to have the knack and the interest. 'We're going to be doctors like Davy,' she announced proudly when they'd done something with some of the willow bark that Bekah's grandfather had told them about.

'Don't be stupid, child!' snapped Mother. 'Medicine's for men. You just need to know how to care for your babies and your family when you have one!'

'But..!' wailed Elspeth.

'Shush now,' said Lowri quietly. Always the peacemaker, she took out her needles and bent dutifully over her knitting. This was no time to fight battles.

There were too many bodies everywhere. When I went to get more wool I had to step over Callum's legs. When I went to fetch milk from the dairy, I had to pass Callum's chair. If I went upstairs, downstairs or outside … My book was safe under my mattress, wrapped in a petticoat. Not even Callum would investigate there, would he? But he kept looking at me, as if he was only waiting for the right time…

We prayed even more than usual - morning and evening and Grace before meals turned into lengthy prayers. In between the out loud prayers I said some prayers in my head. For the angel. For Fin. Mother made us all read the Bible out loud in turn. 'To give us faith and courage and remind us we are safe in the Lord,' she said. Though I could see she was terrified. To be honest, we all were. But by Friday the wind had begun to ease though the rain still slashed down, cold and hard.

'A good thing,' said Father. 'It will wash away the black tar perhaps.'

I longed for fresh air, however wet and still smelling of oil and tar, and freedom to move more than a few steps without tripping over a brother, sister or dog and to be out from under Callum's constant gaze. 'I'm going to the polytunnels to see what state they're in,' I said, grabbing an ancient hooded coat from the hall and diving out into the rain before anyone could stop me.

The rain sheeted down on me, icy cold. But it was sharp and fresh so by the time I got to the polytunnels, even though rain was streaming down my face, my skirt was soaked and my feet squelchy with mud, I didn't care.

Inside the large tunnels was chaos. Many of the sheets had been whipped away in the wind, pots had been smashed, seedlings and soil lay scattered on the ground. Some were so coated with the black dust that they would be unusable but some were worth the effort of rescuing.

'Were you desperate to get out too?' laughed Bekah who was equally wet and bedraggled, her cheeks pink and the rain dripping off curls that had escaped from her headscarf.

'Oh yes, what with my mother glaring at me and Callum leering, I thought I was going mad!'

Above us men were making rough repairs to the least damaged polytunnel.

'Let's see what we can rescue,' I said, 'and bring it all in here.' For hours we staggered back and forth with pots, re-planted small seedlings, swept broken pots into the corner and oily soil into a heap. Some plants had just borne first fruits – tiny green tomatoes, small lettuces, gooseberries and tiny carrots no bigger than your finger. Those we could re-plant we did. Some of the others I pushed deep into my skirt pockets...

Gradually, more girls came out to join us, as the lads clambered up ladders and hammered the billowing sheets of covering into place. The work slowed a bit. This could be my best chance. Smaller children arrived with jugs of water and milk to keep the workers going.

While Bekah and another girl were re-potting the last of the tomatoes, I walked purposefully towards the back of the polytunnel. As I slid out of the battered entrance, I picked up a can of milk that someone had left there. They'd think they'd misplaced it in the chaos. Then I rushed out into the wind and rain and down the path to the beach. I had to see if the angel stranger was still there. If he was alright…

The sea crashed over the stepping-stones. I could hardly find them beneath my feet and the force of the waves nearly pushed me into the angry water. The rain whipped so hard across my face that I couldn't see. I clambered down the rocks my feet scrabbling to grip the wet surface. In the otter cove I could see all the signs of storm - heaps of seaweed, bits of drift wood and dead birds, their feathers covered with the oil that had come on the wind and brought them down. Too late for them to be cleaned by the rain. Head down against the torrent, I struggled up to the beach and into the shelter of the cave. As my eyes adjusted to the sudden darkness I heard a strange low noise. A groan.

I hesitated. No one knew I was here. No one would come to my aid. Who or what could be in there? Could be someone dangerous. Could be an animal. People still talked of mysterious black panthers that stalked the countryside. 'Big cat,' I thought ludicrously to myself, remembering Shenavar's English text book and cheered up.

'Hello?' I said, going a few steps further into the cave, so the light narrowed and the noise of the rain and sea seemed duller and far away. 'Hello?' The cave, normally dry and clean, smelt of damp and rotting seaweed, of the oil from the black cloud, of dead birds and fish. I didn't want to stay and turned to go.

The groan again. My heart thudding, I went forward a few more steps – checking over my shoulder that I could run out again quickly if need be. Then I saw a gleam of gold in the dim light in the back of the cave. A sudden whirl of movement. A giant shadow leapt across the cave, soaring around the walls and into the blackness.

Then the angel was in front of me, his eyes wild, his face pale and in his hand a knife which he pointed at my throat.

Listen. *'You make plans. Then the world changes in an instant. What use are plans then? You can only start from where you are.'*

Chapter 22

Lucas

'**A**rrgh..!' I gasped, trying hard not to scream.

The blade gleamed in the light from the cave entrance. It was thin, sharp, dangerous and inches away from my skin.

Instinctively, I stepped back. Then stopped. It was like dealing with an unpredictable animal. I knew I mustn't startle him. So I stood my ground and gazed at him as calmly as I could. It was the angel right enough.

But he was changed utterly. His golden skin was pale and clammy, his face gaunt. One arm was bound up, the strapping filthy. He must have been hiding here all the time of the black cloud and the storms. No wonder he looked so grim.

My heart thudded but I held his gaze. He looked at me suspiciously. Even if I'd wanted to run, I couldn't. I was frozen to the spot. But I carried on looking into his face. Gradually, his eyes grew calmer, almost questioning. He lowered the knife a fraction, seemed to relax a little. I realised I'd been holding my breath all this time and let out a deep sigh. Then I remembered Shenavar's book and swallowed.

'My name is Amity,' I said carefully in English.

His face lit up and he started talking rapidly. Obviously trying to tell me something very important. But of course I didn't understand a word. No mention of big dogs or small cats…

I shrugged to show I didn't understand and again said 'My name is Amity.' I stood very still, gazing into his eyes.

He nodded. Slowly, his eyes staring into mine, he tucked the knife into the waistband of his trousers. 'My name' he said, pointing at himself, 'is Lucas.'

'Lucas,' I said carefully, trying the name in my mouth. 'Lucas.'

We gazed at each other for a moment. Then I remembered and passed him the can of milk. He seized the can with his one good hand, cradling it with his strapped up arm. Then drank the milk down in one long swallow. I wondered how long it was since he'd last eaten.

'Thank you,' he said slowly, to make sure I understood. 'Thank you.'

I scrabbled in my pocket and pulled out the young strawberries, carrots and tomatoes I'd rescued from the smashed plants in the polytunnels. He smiled and ate them quickly. He had wonderful white teeth. Not a bit like Callum's.

Now my eyes had got used to the gloom I could see something strange at the back of the cave and realised it must be the *sat.com* box. He'd opened it. It looked like one of the computers or TV sets that Mother broke up to use the glass screen as a window.

I stared at it. He pointed to me and then the box, with a questioning look. He gabbled again and I looked blank. 'But if you're asking if I left it there, then yes,' I nodded and pointed outside to the sand. He nodded again and said some more.

'Oh! there's no point. I can't understand!' I said, in agonies at the hopelessness of it.

Then Lucas pounced on a gull feather, smoothed a patch of sand in the grey light near the cave entrance and started drawing a picture, looking up at me every now and then with his bright eyes to see if I understood. It was a bird. I could see that much. But it didn't mean anything until he drew a twig in the bird's beak.

An olive branch. A dove. The universal and eternal sign of peace. When Noah's Ark had floated on the floods Noah sent the dove out and it came back with an olive branch so Noah knew they were near dry land and the battle was over. Peace. How did I make him understand than I'd understood?

Obvious really. The story of Noah and his ark and the flood ends with God sending a rainbow as a sign of His promise that all will be well. I took the gull's feather from Lucas and next to the dove, I sketched a rough stripy rainbow. Not exactly great art but it would have to do.

Lucas looked and his face lit up as he smiled and nodded. We had no words but we understood each other. He held out his hand and I shook it. Friends.

Then he coughed and shivered.

'I must go,' I said. 'But I'll come back.'

I don't know if he understood but he retreated to the back of the cave. I turned and waved and then went back out into the storm and battled my way back home. When I got back Mother had taken the little ones to the community centre for baths. A chance too good to miss. I raced around the house gathering what I needed.

I took the old blanket off my bed - no one but me would miss it - and wrapped it round my shoulders with the old waterproof on top. I looked fatter and bulkier but in the torrential rain no one was going to notice. From the kitchen I took what food I thought might not be missed. Then, in the small room off the dairy, which we called Lowri's still room, I gazed at her pots and jars of herbs and potions and took a small jar of the willow bark mixture that I had helped to make. Then I snatched a can of milk and ran.

I bundled them up with my bag and towel - so I could go straight to the baths as if I'd just come from home - and slipped around the back of the polytunnels and another short steep path to the stepping stones and otter beach I ran all the way and slid down the bank on my bum so I was soaked to the skin and out of breath when I got to the cave entrance and slowed down and stopped, suddenly nervous, rain trickling down the back of my neck, my bare feet streaked with mud and blue with cold

'Lucas?' I called out softly 'Lucas?'

He came towards me slowly from the back of the cave. When he saw me and recognised me, he smiled. I unwrapped my heavy coat, pushed the blanket, the food and the medicine towards him and went. There was no time to try and explain. No words either.

But at the entrance of the cave I turned and looked back. Lucas was still smiling at me and the warmth of his smile gave the gloomy cave a golden glow.

Listen. *'At first the world opened up and there was a bit of coming and going between us and Mainland. Some people left to see if they could find any family left alive. But the journey was always difficult. There was talk of building a proper jetty but nothing came of it. Soon only the men from Mainland were crossing. It was as if they wanted to keep us here, apart from the world. Sometimes I felt I was living in some awful experiment.*

'Meanwhile the island was in a religious fervour, whipped up by the incomers. But with so many men suddenly on the island it was useful for mothers to have a way of controlling their daughters. They tried to outdo each other in piety and modesty. Ridiculous really. But it gave more power to the men and took it from the women.'

Chapter 23

A Plan

It was days before I could get away again. Mother kept me furiously busy with all the tiresome jobs - digging our own small vegetable patch in the torrential rain, cleaning the pig sty, mending Callum's britches - yuk and yuk again - and scrubbing the house, inside and out to try and get rid of the tarry, oily film that spread everywhere.

'You shall not eat the bread of idleness,' she said.

I'd just finished scrubbing the kitchen with our home made soap made of pig fat and ashes, my skirt and apron were soaking wet, my knees creaking and my hands red raw. I was rocking back on my heels, wringing out the old floor cloth for one last time, thinking that at last I'd finished, when Callum came in his big patched work boots and walked across the floor leaving a trail of thick muddy boot prints.

'Oh sorry,' he said, grinning as he looked down at me, giving me a fine view of his yellow teeth. 'I didn't see you there. Read any good books lately?' And he nudged the bucket with his toe, spilling dirty oily water in every corner of the kitchen again.

I longed to hurl the heavy bucket at his head and wipe that stupid sly grin of his face. Instead, I said not a word, just put the bucket upright and started mopping up with the floor cloth. No way was I going to give him the joy of thinking he'd upset me.

Mother was barely speaking to me, other than to issue more orders. I was paying the price for everything I seemed to have done wrong lately - not marrying Idris Mordecai, standing up to Fin, being rude to the elders at Shenavar's funeral. But I didn't care, I'd say it all again. I just wish more people had heard me.

What was there for me on the island any more? It was clear I'd have to get away. On days like that when Callum was being vile or Mother was shouting at me, it was all that kept me sane. When the Traders came again, I would persuade Xander to take me. He would do it for his grandfather's sake, for Shenavar's. I didn't know what the world was like but if nothing else I would have a chance to find out. Xander had said that people were beginning to live normal lives in a small way. I could find out for myself, I would work hard. There would be somewhere I could fit in. I started to dream about what I would need, what I could take. It was just a matter of time.

'What are you smiling at, you stupid girl?' demanded Callum. I ignored him and carried on mopping the floor without a word. At least that meant Callum didn't have the satisfaction of seeing me upset. That was a sort of triumph, wasn't it?

Later Lowri took one look at my hands and said 'Ooh they look sore. I've some new salve that will help. I made a mixture using lanolin from the sheep wool and some mint.'

I followed her into still room and she opened a big jar of yellow ointment and scooped a dollop onto my hands.

'Mmm, it stings and then I can feel it soaking in,' I said, rubbing my hands together and spreading the salve up my arms and elbows. Already I could feel it soothing the blisters and tiny cuts.

'That's odd,' said Lowri, still standing with the open jar.

'What?'

'That preparation of willow bark when we were all indoors when the black cloud came, the one you ground the bark for, I haven't used it or given it to anyone, but one of the jars has gone.'

'Ah,' I said, concentrating on rubbing the ointment into my finger nails as if my life depended on it and trying not to look at Lowri, 'perhaps someone had need of it.'

'No doubt,' said Lowri. 'But they should have asked. It could be dangerous for some people. And to take it without asking…'

'Maybe they really, *really* had need of it, Lowri. And maybe they didn't ask because….because maybe it would be better if no one knew.'

'Amity! What are you up to?' My sister looked at me sharply. I'd never realised how much she looked like our mother.

'Nothing, absolutely nothing. Not for you to know about.' I reached out and took another scoop of the salve.

'Is it something to do with Fin?' asked Lowri, still clutching the jar. 'Have you seen him again? Is he in trouble? Or is it…I don't know, is it poor Lizzie and her baby?'

'No,' I said sadly, 'It's nothing to do with Fin. Well, I don't think so. I haven't seen him since he rode off on his fine horse. Nor Lizzie since the day of the shaming. I hope she's alright.'

'Then what is it? Who is it?'

'I'm not telling you Lowri. Partly because I promised someone. But mainly because it could cause all sorts of problems for you. And I don't want that. Just don't worry about the willow bark, please?'

She shrugged and turned away but looked so hurt that I felt miserable because I've always been close to Lowri and now the angel, Lucas had come between us. But better that than tell her about him. That would be bad news for us all.

Then an accident of fate helped us.

'There now,' said Mother when she came back from the baths. 'If Prudence Prendergast and her daughter Clemency, haven't both had babies on the same day. Prudence's came last night and Clemency's an hour ago - nearly a month early so she and the babe need some looking after.'

Clemency had no sisters, just a house full of brothers so mother and daughter were in no position to care for each other.

'Ah well, I expect I'd better get over to the house and see what I can do for them all,' said Mother, who was very close to Prudence. 'You girls can look after things here. Make sure you do things properly!'

So now she was spending a lot of time with Prudence her daughter and their babies, leaving me and Lowri to look after our family.

'Perfect!' I said to Lowri. 'I have things I must attend to. And I'm sure you would like a chance to talk with Cornelius – I just happen to know he's working on his own in the top field. You go and see Cornelius and I'll look after the little ones. And when you come back….'

'What are you up to Amity?' she asked suspiciously. 'Is this anything to do with the missing potion? Who was it for? And why can't you tell me?' Her expression was hard. She knew I was keeping something from her and didn't like it. We'd never had secrets between us. It made me feel heavy-hearted. Why was life so complicated?

'I will do, Lowri, I promise. But not just yet? Please? It really is important.'

She still looked unconvinced. Oh I needed so much for her to agree! 'Lowri, all you need to know is that I'm doing nothing wrong. Honestly. As God is my witness,' I said, putting my hand on my heart.

'Really?' She looked unconvinced.

'Really. And wouldn't you like to spend a little time with Cornelius?' I said as persuasively as I could.

There was a pause. 'It's nothing really…wrong…is it Amity?' she asked. 'Nothing .. sinful?'

I laughed. 'No, I promise you.'

She shrugged. 'Well alright then…'

'Cornelius. Top field.' I said and she turned and went.

It worked like a dream. I put baby Liam in his little wheeled walker and he pushed himself back and forth, chewing on an oatcake as I dashed around the house doing the cleaning, sorting out washing. I made a big pan of mutton stew for everyone to have when they came in. I even churned the butter – and it worked straightaway. So often the milk goes sloshing on for ever, but today it seemed to get straight to the soft thump thump thump of butter in minutes. It must have meant God was on my side, mustn't it?

As soon as Lowri came back I gave her precisely two minutes to tell me how wonderful Cornelius Blackwood was (His perfect smile, his lovely laugh, his eyes that are grey with just a fleck of green) and then off I dashed.

Wrapped in my pocket I had some food and some more of the willow bark mixture and rolled up tightly in my knitting sheath I had Shenavar's home-made English text book. I was determined to talk to Lucas.

Listen. *We spoke Celtic at home among ourselves and in school we learned French, Spanish and Italian. But we all spoke English too. Everywhere you went in the world you found people who could speak English. With good will and a bit of English, you could talk to almost anyone, anywhere.'*

Chapter 24

The Magic Cave

So started the most amazing week of my life.

Every day Lucas and I snatched an hour or so together. Magic hours. Outside the world seemed to be racing towards another war. My mother was barely speaking to me except to issue instructions. Lowri and I hadn't exactly fallen out but there was a distance between us, which made me feel sad. Callum was making my life as miserable as he could. As for Fin, I had to try and make myself forget him...

But every day when I was with Lucas for that short time I felt as though I'd stepped into another world, a world of light and colour, different from anything I'd ever known - different even from what I'd imagined when listening to Shenavar's stories.

I knew nothing about Lucas or his life and could hardly imagine his world. We didn't even speak each other's language. Yet as we sat together on the rocks at the entrance to the cave, looking out to sea, I knew this was important, this was the greatest adventure of my life.

The first time I went down after Lowri and I struck our deal, he was so pleased to see me. He came cautiously out of the cave, his knife in his good hand, but immediately stopped and smiled, a smile that went even to his eyes. 'Hello Amity,' he said carefully. He already looked much better thanks to the food and Lowri's medicine. And although his arm was awkward and clearly uncomfortable it seemed bearable.

'Here's some food,' I said, handing him the package, 'and some more willow bark mixture.' As he took them, he put his hand on top of mine for a second. I held my breath. In the dampness of the cave I could feel the gentle warmth of his skin and a strange connection between us. Only when he moved his hand again did I breathe out again.

He spoke very little Celtic but we used the little dictionary at the back of Shenavar's book to help us and a lot of mime and drawing. So when I looked at the *sat.com* box which sat just outside the cave entrance, a tiny light blinking on its screen, Lucas mimed someone searching high and low, peering through the distance and then finding the box. At first I didn't understand what he meant, so he did it all again, exaggerating his actions, and making me laugh. But I understood that somehow it would guide people to him.

He nursed his arm and grimaced in pain, mimed galloping on a horse and almost falling off. I imagined how that ride must have been with Fin but I had no idea of where Fin had taken him, or what he'd done... Then Lucas smiled and looked relieved so someone must have strapped it up and helped him. I'm glad Fin organised that at least.

153

'But why did you escape?' I asked. 'And how?' I pointed to the boat and mimed paddling it.

He could never have got across the channel from Mainland, not in that little boat. Not paddling with one arm, but I had no idea where he'd been kept there. Lucas pointed along the shore and stretched his arms wide so all I could guess was that he'd been kept on the other side of the island, near the makeshift jetty used by the Engineers. Islanders weren't encouraged to go near there so I knew little about it.

Lucas pointed at the *sat.com* box and I knew that meant he needed to get home.

'Somehow that will help you?' I asked.

I'm not sure if he understood, but he pointed into the distance and nodded. As he ate the food I'd brought and swallowed the willow bark mixture, I sat beside him, pointing out words and sentences from the book. If he spoke English then maybe he can't have come from the White Star states.

On the floor of the cave he drew a map. It showed the island at the top and other islands and Mainland, then England and Europe and the huge lands to the north and east of Europe. With the feather he marked a cross in the middle of England, a few miles inland, where a big river came in from the sea, and pointed to himself.

So he was from what used to be England, part of Outland. The land the Elders told us was full of infidels and unbelievers and children of the Devil. I remembered the battered book I'd read. Did those palaces and castles still exist? Was the grass so green the lakes so clean? Lucas didn't look much a child of the Devil to me. He looked fierce sometimes, and determined but he was gentle too and kind.

'But you want peace?' I said and drew a rainbow

again to make sure.

He nodded and then over in the vast north eastern reaches of Outland he scribbled angrily with the feather, then drew fierce lines coming towards England, Mainland and the Island.

I searched Shenavar's book. 'War?' I pointed.

He nodded and looked grim.

'Well, we can't get very far without words,' I said and went back to Shenavar's book with its simple questions and answers.

I beamed at him. 'See, we can communicate after all,' I said. 'What's it like where you live? Are there lots of people there? How do you live? Do you farm? Can you grow things?'

He smiled but looked baffled, not understanding my stream of questions. But he gestured at the food I'd brought him and pointed to the word 'Plenty' and looked at me questioningly.

'Yes,' I said. 'We have plenty of food. The Hungry Years are a distant memory only for the old people. No one on the island need go hungry now. We have meat and milk and vegetables, more now that the black clouds don't come as often and now we even sometimes have fish from the rivers.'

He pointed to the word 'house' and then 'everyone.'

I laughed and nodded. *Of course* every one had a house! Certainly many had been destroyed in storms, but there were still plenty of empty ones for when we needed more and the ruins of others if we needed to build.

'Fire?'

Yes, we dug peat. I mimed warming myself in front of a fire. There was plenty of peat. And clean water from deep underground, untainted by the black clouds.

He drew a picture of a wind turbine so he knew we had some electricity. I mimed using a machine and showers and washing and he smiled his understanding.

'You live in Paradise,' he said.

Paradise was a word I didn't understand then.

He pointed to another word. 'Lucky.'

We were. I knew that. We were lucky to have survived in the first place and even luckier to still be here with lots of young people. We had proper houses and plenty of food and electricity to make our lives easier. We had a community that worked. We were a lot luckier than people in other parts of the world. But…but…*but* … Maybe Mother was right and to want more from life was to be ungrateful. Well, if so, then put me down as greedy.

So Lucas and I sat a bit closer and shared Shenavar's book. We read out sentences to each other, our fingers following the words. Sometimes our hands touched as we turned a page. I felt a small shock every time his skin brushed mine, but he didn't even seem to notice. I was embarrassed by my fingers, red raw from the work I'd been doing. Lucas's were long and strong. I tried not to gaze at him too much as I explained the Celtic way of saying things and he repeated them carefully. Then he said the English and I repeated after him.

Despite the desperateness of his situation, he was never downcast. Not when I was there anyway. Even when I couldn't understand what he was saying there seemed to be a smile in his voice. I couldn't stay too long as I mustn't be missed. Neither did I want to make people suspicious and maybe find him.

But each day the minutes flew by more quickly, his smile seemed warmer, our hands seemed to touch more often. Every new word we learned of each other's languages brought us closer together. I felt… well, each day it was harder to leave him.

One day something strange happened. We were doing the numbers. He was pointing to the figures in the book and saying carefully 'One, two three, four, five…'

'Once I caught a fish alive!' I sang suddenly, not knowing where the words came from or even what they meant. They'd just leapt from my tongue without my knowing.

Surprised, Lucas laughed delightedly. 'Six, seven, eight, nine ten…'

'Then I let them go again.' More words, from where?

'Why did you let them go?' he sang again, But the words had left me. I had no more. What had happened? Where had these words been hiding in my head?

Now Lucas was taking my hands. 'Where did you learn those?' But I couldn't tell him. Even if I had the words in English I couldn't tell him. He pointed to the words 'baby' and 'sing' in the book, so I knew that I was singing nursery rhymes.

Excited now, his face alight - he was clearly intrigued by this sudden odd knowledge, he was singing more little rhymes at me, clearly meant for babies. They meant nothing at all to me. Just meaningless noise. Each time I shook my head he looked a little disappointed. He was clearly racking his brains to remember one more rhyme.

'Bah bah black sheep,' he started

'Have you any wool?' I sang triumphantly, looking at him to see if it was right.

His face lit up again and I felt as though I'd passed a very difficult test.

But why did I know these rhymes? The only one

who would have sing them to me was Shenavar but in that case she would have sung them to my brothers and sisters too. And I can't consciously remember ever hearing them.

But someone had sung them to me long ago and they'd stayed in my mind ever since…

Sometime I would have to think about that. But now Lucas was getting anxious. He kept looking out to sea, waiting to be rescued. Maybe his *sat.com* box wasn't giving out a signal after all. Or maybe no one had heard it. Or maybe they'd heard it and weren't coming to get him.

Every time we heard the distant throb of a motorboat, he leapt to his feet and went to look and then had to fling himself down on the sand again behind the rocks as he realised it was an Engineers' boat, out patrolling the seas and probably looking for him.

I wondered if he'd ever escape. Or if at some point he would have to leave the cave and risk his life out on the island. As I took over from Lowri and baked another batch of oatcakes and made the soup for supper, a little tune kept humming through my head 'One, two, three, four five…'

Listen. *Some people couldn't cope. The isolation destroyed their minds. The rest of us concentrated on the here and now. It didn't do to think too much. But sometimes… I had a dress I'd worn before the wars to my sister's wedding. I couldn't bear it because it reminded me of my family, all gone and of happier times, of dancing and laughter and a boy I loved… Eventually I cut it up for a quilt for my baby's bed so I could wrap the happy memories around him.*

Chapter 25

Learning to Dance Again

The smell of oil again. Heavy and sickly, it suddenly filled the air as I battled to hang up heavy wet blankets on the washing line outside the community centre. Mother's idea to keep me busy, of course. At least she was still busy helping Prudence Prendergast and her daughter. Lowri was taking her turn as part of the deal and had slipped off somewhere to be with Cornelius Blackwood.

'What's that noise?' asked Bekah who'd come out with her own basket of washing. 'Is it thunder? Not.. gunfire? It's getting closer!'

She turned and ran back indoors, leaving the basket of washing tumbled on the floor. But there was no black oily cloud. Just strange vehicles trundling through the centre of the village. No horses. Just trucks moving of their own accord with a man at a steering wheel looking out through the window.

I'd never seen trucks before, not trucks that

moved. There were a few rotting away, abandoned when they broke down and were finally beyond repair. Now the only vehicles we had were pulled by horse or donkey. The only petrol now was on Mainland, closely guarded and rarely used.

I hadn't realised they made so much noise.

A whole convoy of trucks was wrecking the silence, making the earth move and filling the air with that all too familiar smell of oil as they trundled without stopping on through our village. They seemed like big trampling beasts with a life-force of their own, trailing black clouds.

In the back, the trucks were full of young men, Engineers, I supposed, leaning out, each armed with a fearsome looking gun. Bekah came to the door of the laundry to look out, but wouldn't step over the threshold again. Some of the children rushed over to look at these strange beasts but their mothers dragged them back and hurried them indoors. Then they peeped warily out of the windows, fear in their eyes, wondering what was going on.

The Elders came out to greet the men in charge of the Engineers. Mrs Chief Elder, Priscilla at her side, bustled up very importantly with keys. Soon teams of men started loading the trucks with supplies from the community kitchen. Back and forth they went with meat from the freezer, churns of milk and sacks of vegetables. Then the trucks roared into life and lurched along our bumpy roads and out of the village, leaving the dirty smell of exhaust fumes behind them.

'What's happening?' asked Elspeth when I got home. 'Is there another war starting?'

'I don't know,' I said, feeling hopeless and helpless.

The threat of war pressed down on us all, brought down by the sight of the trucks and the sound of the Engineers' boats out near the rigs and the boom of distant guns. There was threat in the muttered conversations between the men on the benches outside the community centre, in the way that they, even my father, took their guns and went out on patrol. The threat was everywhere, choking our lives just like the big black clouds.

Of course I feared for my family and friends and our life on the island. But when I thought of Lucas the fear was sudden and sharp, like the stab of a knife that made it hard to breathe. How could his hiding place stay safe with all these patrols watching the sea and shore?

Restless, anxious, I could hardly bear to wait to get back to him, to our strange and wonderful life in the cave. In the that small space he'd opened up a world for me. The narrow cave with its rocky walls and sandy floor was the gateway to a world of new ideas, where people had the freedom to live differently. And I was intrigued about how I'd found deep in my brain, some rhymes meant for English babies. I was greedy to learn more.

It couldn't last, of course.

'I think those new babies are beginning to thrive at last,' said Mother as she was leaving the house early in the morning. 'Prudence and her mother will be coping soon, I think after today I can come back here and get this house back in shape.'

'Haven't the girls done a good job?' asked Father, as he laced up his patched old work boots and pulled on his work jacket. 'Everything seems to have been just fine.'

Mother just sniffed. There was clearly no pleasing her. But I watched in horror as Mother filled a basket with food for Prudence and her family. This could be the last day I could easily get to see Lucas. As Lowri saw to the animals, I got the little ones breakfasted and dressed as quickly as I could so they squawked in indignation.

But they were ready, Lowri was back. I could go.

I was fastening my headscarf, peering in the tiny bit of broken mirror by the back door when I saw a shadow loom over my reflection. Callum. His face appeared in the blotchy surface beside mine. He was standing there behind me in the kitchen, leaning against the wall just watching me...

'Haven't you got work to do ?' I snapped, twirling round. 'Father will be waiting. He's long gone. You'll have to run to catch him up.'

Callum didn't rush. 'I'm not working with your father today,' he said, 'I have work of my own to do at my house.'

'*Your* house?' I was baffled. 'Oh you mean your parents' house.'

I knew he went over there regularly to keep the house in good repair. Please God let him be moving out to it soon. But he just grinned as he eased himself away from the wall as though he had all the time in the world and then went out, sauntering down the path, looking particularly pleased with himself.

'Ohh!' I said to Lowri, 'one day I'm going to *throw* something at Callum. But now,' I went on, picking up my collecting bag as though I were gathering plants and mosses for dyes 'I must be out. I shan't be long.' I grinned. 'Then it will be your turn.'

I filled the collecting bag with food. Then, as I

went, I had a thought and snatched up the lion from the Noah's ark. I left the village from the opposite end from the shore. I picked some mosses and a few celandines, daisies and purple vetches so I had something genuine in my collecting bag. Then I doubled back and zig zagged so much that if you'd asked four different people which way I was going, they'd have given four different directions.

'Hello' said Lucas, appearing out of the shadows at the back of the cave. He looked so much better. His eyes were brighter, his skin clear. I marvelled at my little sister's skill with medicines.

'Engineers,' I blurted out straightaway. 'Trucks' I made brrrmm brrrmm noises and mimed shooting.

Lucas nodded and seemed unsurprised. Or even particularly bothered. He glanced at his *sat.com* box then pointed out to sea where we could see patrol boats. There were three boats out there. I'd never seen more than one at a time ever before. Lucas shrugged. He seemed confident that he would be rescued. I couldn't see how. Or how they would get past the patrols.

I unpacked the food and Shenavar's English word book. As I took out some apples, stored from last year, a bit small but not tasting too much of oil, the little wooden lion tumbled out. I picked it up and showed it to Lucas.

'What noise does a lion make?' I asked. And when Lucas looked blank, I said, as Father had 'Meeow?'

Lucas laughed and shook his head. Then he held up his arms in front of him like big paws about to pounce, shook his long hair like a mane and roared. The noise bounced and echoed all around the cave filling the space with the fierceness of the sound and I jumped back, surprised and laughing, my back against the chill of the rocky wall.

Oh, it seemed so *right*. We knew from the Bible that the lion was a mighty beast. Of course he would have a mighty roar. It fitted perfectly and made Father's meeow seem both silly and sad. Now I had a tiny crumb of knowledge about the world outside that I hadn't had before. That was as good as a present.

'And how big's a giraffe?' I asked. Giraffe wasn't in Shenavar's word list. I tried to draw the creature as I saw it on the little wooden toy.

'Giraffe!' Lucas and pointed up to the very roof of the cave.

'Really? That tall! But how do you know? Have you seen a lion or a giraffe? Have you heard one?'

He was looking in the word book but couldn't find what he wanted. '*Films*' he said, but I didn't know what that meant. He pointed instead to '*book*'.

'Oh books,' I said sadly. 'We have no books.' I shook my head to make it clear. 'Only the Bible.'

Lucas looked astonished and pointed again at 'book'.

'No, no books.'

'*Learn?*' he pointed.

'*Talk,*' I pointed to the word.

When the Elders had taken Shenavar's books they had taken not just a gateway into the world and imagination but the chance of knowledge. It was the Bible or nothing. All the knowledge we had was handed down by word of mouth, practical skills or half-remembered stories and theories and the few dog-eared books on very practical subjects.

It meant that our knowledge could never get any

deeper or wider. Without books or other people from other places, all we would ever know was whatever we had ever known. Less really, as we were bound to forget stuff. There was no chance for our knowledge to grow, no chance for anything new.

Maybe for the boys who went to the Engineers, but not for the rest of us. And the things we wanted to know, there was no way to find out. I didn't even know what I wanted to know – that's how little I knew. I had no words to say any of this to Lucas, no way of being able to tell him how greedy I was to know more. But I roared like a lion and felt suddenly powerful as Lucas laughed.

Now Lucas was pointing to *"music"* and miming as if he were playing a guitar, then a flute. I mimed playing the fiddle like Father and then throwing it to the ground and smashing it. Lucas looked puzzled again. *"Dance?"* I played the fiddle again and hummed Father's dance tune and skipped a few steps on the sandy floor. Lucas smiled as if he understood, then held out his good hand to me.

'I'm not sure,' I said, partly of what the elders said about dancing but mainly because of my rough red hands in his long, cool fingers. But now he had picked up the tune and was humming it, looking at me, his eyes sparkling. So of course I took his hand.

Up and down the narrow cave we skipped, as I had danced with Fin many years before. And we sang all the time, the happy tune that Father hummed when he forgot to be solemn. Up and down and round. Oh it was wonderful to feel the freedom of the movement, the skipping steps. So free, so happy – so *alive*. My headscarf slipped off and I didn't care. I just flung it towards my bag. My hair swirled over my shoulders and across my face so I couldn't see.

We joined hands - or hand, in Lucas's case, being careful of his bad arm - and unjoined, twirled and skipped. Lucas was quick to learn the steps, to follow my lead. His feet were nimble and he laughed as he followed me. He held his head high, his long golden hair swished around him. He was elegant, magical, a creature from another world and when we danced near the cave entrance the sun streamed in so he seemed to glow with energy.

Finally I collapsed, laughing, unable to sing and dance at the same time. 'I've run out of breath,' I said, leaning back to perch on the shelf of rock, knowing my face was bright pink, and clutching my side as I had a stitch. I was conscious of my hair loose over my shoulders, stray strands across my burning face.

Lucas perched beside me for a moment, his hands on his knees as he too got his breath back. We glanced at each other and laughed and although we didn't have many words between us, it felt very companionable. Special.

Some of the flowers had spilled out of my collecting bag. Lucas picked them up and as I pushed my hair back from my face, Lucas tucked a cowslip behind my ear. Then a bit awkwardly as he was using only one hand, he pushed some celandines into my hair, then a tendril of young ivy that he twisted round and placed gently on my head. He stood so close to me he smelt of sea and sand, of the spray of the waves. As I stood there, hardly breathing he tucked yellow celandines and dandelions and purple vetch into this make-shift crown. I could feel it balanced gently on my head, the flower stalks entwined with my hair. Lucas stepped back a bit and smiled at his handiwork and then at me, a wonderful dancing smile that seemed to wrap itself around me.

Then he started to sing, a strange slow song with a lilting melody that curled around the cave into its very corners and crevices. Very beautiful. He bowed to me, very courteously as though he were asking me to dance. Then he placed one of my hands on his shoulder, balanced his bad arm around my waist and held my other hand and pulled me close to him. I wasn't sure at first. I'd never been that close to any boy except Fin but then as he sang in his loud, strong voice, I followed his lead.

This dance was different from anything I ever knew. We dipped and swayed around the cave. At first I stumbled and fell and stood on Lucas' feet. I put my hand up to protect my crown of flowers but it stayed safely caught in my hair. Soon my feet had the rhythm of his singing and I could tell when we were going and we moved like one person around the cave, as if we were hardly touching the ground at all, but drifting through air. I remembered long ago stories that Shenavar had told me, of the girl in wonderful shoes who goes to the ball and dances with the prince.

I laughed at the thought. Lucas looked at me as if to ask what was so funny.

'I'm happy,' I said, a huge smile on my face. 'I'm happy.'

Even if he didn't know the word, it would have been hard not guess what I meant. Then he took one of the shells and drew in the sand again, in among our footprints. He drew the rough map that had showed his home. Then he took my hand and pointed to it, to him and then to me. 'Come with me,' he said and smiled.

'To your home?' I wasn't sure if I'd understood. But he nodded.

In a second a whole world opened up I front of me, a new life in a new place, with Lucas. Oh. My heart raced. But then I came back down to earth.

'It's going to be hard enough to get you away from here. We can never both go,' I said. And Fin, I didn't know if I could leave the hope of Fin.

I'm not sure if Lucas understood but he scribbled out the map as if it had been a daft idea. And as I puzzled over what it all meant, he pulled me closer and danced me around the cave again.

I forgot I was wearing my heavy long skirt and my rough blouse and that my hands were red and blistered with work. My feet were dirty and bare and calloused and scuffing up the map in the damp sand on the floor of the cave. None of that mattered.

For those few moments in Lucas's arms, I was no longer trapped in drab clothes on the drab island with no hope of anything different. Instead, I felt like the girl in the story. I was in a different world. And it was magical.

Listen. *'Before the wars music was such a part of our lives. We were rarely without it. Sometimes it just cheered us up, made us happy, made our feet itch to dance. Other times it was so powerful, it seemed to run in our blood, take us out of ourselves, to another world.'*

Chapter 26

Davy

I danced up from the beach in a dream, my head full of the lilting tune that Lucas had sung. My scarred feet scuffed up small clouds of sand and dust as I tried to remember the steps. I was in a world of my own as I remembered Lucas's hands holding mine, his arm around my waist, the look in his eyes. Then there was that suggestion I could go with him. Impossible, I know. But he'd asked…

I'd put my headscarf back on but in my collecting bag were the flowers that he'd tucked into my hair that had made me feel so different. Also the little wooden lion that had taken me beyond the island. I had learned something new about the world, about lions and giraffes. And I had learned more about music and dancing.

I didn't bother with my knitting. I didn't care. I swung my collecting bag high with happiness. I didn't bother to look modestly down. I looked up at the sky and the scudding clouds and beamed in happiness. I did a little twirl, my eyes closed, remembering Lucas's arms around me.

I didn't see my mother...

'*What* do you think you're doing, girl?' Her voice hissed in my ear as she grabbed my arm so hard she nearly pulled it out of the socket. 'Can I not even trust you to conduct yourself decently and modestly instead of cavorting through the houses like a hoyden?'

I wasn't sure what a hoyden was but you can be sure Mother didn't think it was anything good.

'Where have you been? What are you thinking of? Can I not go and tend to a friend in need without you running wild?' She was so angry she was nearly spitting at me. She kept hold of my arm and dragged me along so that my feet barely touched the ground until we came to the path that led up to our house and she suddenly slowed. Her face changed. I looked in astonishment as the angry sharp angles seemed to melt away and her eyes filled with hope and excitement. Her pincer grip on my arm loosened and she stopped, staring up at the house.

There was a man standing outside the door talking to Father and Lowri. A young man, taller and broader since I'd last seen him two years ago but still unmistakeably... 'Davy!' My mother picked up her skirts and ran up the path and flung her arms around my brother. 'How are you? When did you come? How long are you here? Oh, let me look at you!'

Davy laughed as he held her hands and Mother looked him up and down. 'Have you eaten? Are you hungry? How long are you here?' I'd never seen her so excited.

'Give the lad a chance, now wife,' said Father, beaming at them both. 'He's just got here.'

The little ones looked baffled as they watched this new arrival. Most of them couldn't remember him and even Bryn was suddenly shy. Lowri shooed them all into the house. Then Davy looked at me. 'Amity!' He let go one of his hands from Mother's and reached out to me. I hugged him. It was so good to see him again.

'I haven't got long, Mother,' he said. 'We're based at the far side of the island.'

'We?'

'A division of Engineers. Bands from the White Star states have been trying to get onto the oil rigs. We have boats out at sea and Engineers all along the coast. Our company will be based on the cliffs, at the old signalling station. But when we came so close to home, Fin said we could have an hour to visit our families.'

'Fin?' asked Father.

'Yes, he's our commander.'

'Well, well,' said Father. 'As one of the Elect I suppose he would be. The boy's gone far.'

'Yes he has,' said Davy. 'And he's an excellent commander.' But still he looked uncomfortable.

'Well come on Davy, let's go inside and find you something to eat. Look at you, there's nothing on you. You need feeding up.'

As we went in, I whispered to Elspeth and sent her over to Bekah's.

Mother bustled about, cutting chunks of ham and smoked venison, finding some of Davy's favourite chutney to go with it, all of the time constantly looking across at Davy and beaming. She even pretended not to notice that Nutmeg had bounded into the house and was sitting next to Davy, begging for crumbs and licking his hand in between to say welcome home.

As Davy ate he was introduced to all his younger brothers and sisters.

'Have you got guns?' asked Bryn overcoming his shyness at the thought of weaponry.

'Yes and grenades and mortars.'

'Ay,' muttered Father, 'For holy people the Elders are good at killing.'

'There was an ammunition factory on Mainland. It was heavily disguised and defended and so survived,' Davy shrugged. 'Pray God we will not need to use it.'

'Do you think you will?'

'I don't know. Fin says the White Star states are just taking a gamble, testing the water to see how prepared we are. He thinks they are not yet organised or powerful enough to take us. But by God, I wish we'd allied to our neighbours in Outland. We could share our strength and knowledge.'

Father nodded. We knew well enough what he believed.

'There's no one to challenge the Elders,' he said sadly. 'They only ever choose people to join them who think just like them. If they know your views are against them, you'll never get a chance to say how we should live.'

Davy nodded. 'We went to Outland, you know. Me and Fin.'

Mother had finally taken her eyes off Davy and was bustling in the cupboards upstairs looking for shirts she'd made for him and socks she'd knitted, waiting only for the chance to give them to him. Father, Lowry, Bryn and I sat around the table with Davy.

'Tell us about Outland,' I said.

Listen. *Travelling to Mainland was never easy and our new leaders didn't like us going. Then the jetty was damaged in a storm and they never built the proper jetty they promised. So once again, we were virtually isolated. That's how the Elders liked it.'*

Chapter 27

Outland

Davy spread butter thickly on an oatcake and piled a chunk of ham and a dollop of chutney on top and sighed in appreciation. 'There's nothing like island butter,' he said, 'Nothing.' He chewed happily and dropped a piece of ham into Nutmeg's eager jaw.

'Outland?' I said, desperate to hear where he and Fin had been.

Davy finished his oatcake and piled up another but finally started talking. 'There's no clear border between Mainland and Outland. At either side of the country there are deep estuaries and wide rivers. But once you get up into the mountains, it's harder to see. It's more of a No Man's Land between us, stretching maybe ten or twenty miles with no one quite sure where they belong. Maybe six months after we'd started our training Fin and I were on patrol. Even though I was concentrating on medicine I still had to start by doing technical and military training and a share of the patrols. There were half a dozen of on little mountain ponies. Not the big horses that the Elect have but good tough little creatures, ideal for the countryside.'

Lowri, I could see, longed to ask him about the ponies but thankfully, Davy carried on with the story.

'It was getting late in the afternoon and we were heading back for camp when way down in the distance we could see a village, houses, smoke from chimneys. Fin looked at me and grinned. Then he shouted to the others that we would take a look at something and follow them back.'

'Was that allowed?' asked Father.

'Of course not! But it was an adventure! And you know what Fin is like - or was like anyway.' He looked thoughtful for a moment but carried on.

'The village was further than we thought and it was almost dark when we got there. But we knew straightaway it wasn't one of ours.'

'How?' I asked.

'Music. The first thing we heard as we approached was the sound of flutes. The village was surrounded by a high fence and the music floated over the top like smoke so it didn't seem threatening. It was more magical coming out to us from the darkness, as if it could wrap itself inside our heads and around our hearts.

'Then the dogs started barking so we paused our horses. We didn't want to seem threatening or impolite. A man came out and asked our business. I let Fin do the talking. He told them the truth really, that we were from the North, the Celtic Alliance and that we had wandered off from our patrol.'

'Couldn't they have killed you?' gasped Bryn.

'Possibly,' grinned Davy, 'But unlikely. The villages in the borders play a careful game. They are friends with everyone. So they very politely invited us in and someone took care of our horses. I wondered if we'd ever see them again, but there was nothing we could do about it.

'I knew they must have sent scouts out to be sure we weren't hiding a raiding party behind some trees but the man, Edward, took us to his house and his wife gave us soup and bread. Excellent bread so we knew they grew grain and could grind it. While we ate he sent a boy to bring some of the other village men and women to meet us.'

'Women too?'

'Oh yes. It seems women take an equal share in community matters."

'What were they like?' I asked.

'Very decent. We talked for a long time about things were with the Alliance and how things are with them. They would like to join us but don't want to live by our strict rules. One of the men laughed at us and called us "Holy Joes."

'While we were talking they brought us some beer and things got very relaxed and friendly. After a while Fin asked about the flute music we heard. They seemed surprised that we wanted to hear it, knowing our attitude to music, but they played for us and some more people joined and played guitars and fiddles and other instruments. It was good to hear.'

He glanced up at Father. 'I can't believe it's so very wicked.'

Father said nothing.

'By then it was late and dark with heavy rain,' Davy went on. 'So they pressed us to stay.'

'Do they have electricity?' asked Lowri 'Cattle? Animals?'

'Yes, it seems some have electricity, using water power. But not everyone has and it's not as reliable as ours. They have sheep and pigs and hens and goats. Their cows died and they are trying to get more. But..' and he took another oatcake before continuing, '..they have iron! They have a source of ironstone nearby and have built a furnace to extract it. It's in the early stages but they're confident that they can perfect it.'

'That would be a great breakthrough,' said Father, thinking of how he had to straighten out every bent nail to use again. 'To have iron...'

'The next morning, they showed it to us and explained the process. They were very open about it. Fin understood it better than I did and asked them all sorts of questions which they answered willingly enough. We even helped them carry large stones to complete the furnaces. A few years ago illness swept through the village and took many of their young men so they were glad of our muscles. It was a way of repaying hospitality so we were glad to do it.'

Father nodded in approval. 'Do they have links with other communities?'

'Yes, some. They have markets and exchange goods. But there are warbands too. Mainly further south but they sometimes come raiding and take what they can. That's why they've got that fence and thick thorn hedge. The country seems divided into factions and seems lawless. They can't feel safe and are constantly on guard.

'But the people we met were good folk. On our last night they had a concert for us. There was music and poetry and a sort of play,' Davy explained eagerly. 'The men dressed as women and the women as men.'

Father raised a disapproving eyebrow.

'But it was very funny,' said Davy and looked as though he could tell more but didn't want to risk upsetting Father.

'What did Fin make of it all?' I asked, trying to work out if this was the Fin I knew and loved or the new strange, cold Fin.

'He loved it. It seemed just his sort of thing, especially the...' He gave Father a quick look. '... refreshments they served. As we went back to our beds he was enthusing about the discoveries the villagers had made, especially about the iron and the happiness of the music.'

That was the Fin I knew.

'But the next day when we took our leave he was very quiet, almost as if he regretted that he'd enjoyed himself so much. The next week I went off to start my medical studies properly and I didn't see him for some months. And when I did...'

He shrugged and we all knew what he meant. The strange transformation of someone we thought we knew so well. Davy was as confused about Fin as I was.

'Ah well, Saul on the road to Damascus,' said Father. 'Such conversions are not unusual. God delights to use some of the most unlikely people for his purpose. And those elders love a convert – it's proof of their arguments you see. And such a one as Fin! A real prize for them.

'There's no doubt the lad is highly thought of now and well respected by our leaders.'

So Fin had enjoyed the music in Outland and the plays and the drinking, a taste of freedom and happiness. He would have loved it. He would have danced too. He would have seized that freedom to enjoy life without the disapproval of The Elders who crushed every bit of happiness. I was glad for him that he'd heard the music and seen another way of life. But why had he changed so much? What had happened to him?

Without thinking I groped in my pocket for the little carved otter. But I'd thrown that in the sea days before and with it thrown away all hope of being with Fin again. Instead I found one of the crushed daisies that I'd rescued from the crown that Lucas had made me. I remembered his smile, his hand around my waist, the way he looked at me.

Now Mother came bustling down with a heap of shirts and socks for Davy and a fine pair of leather gloves she'd made from scraps of old ones.

'Thank you, Mother, I'll have need of those.' Davy hugged Mother who held him so tight that even her tiny frame seemed capable of crushing him. Then we heard a light step coming up the path and a hesitant call at the door.

'Bekah?' asked Davy as his face lit up. 'Bekah!'

Bekah came shyly into our kitchen and gazed at Davy as if feasting her eyes on him. After all, it was two years since she'd seen him. Davy untangled himself from Mother and reached his hands out to Bekah.

'Well,' said Father. 'As Davy has to get going now, maybe Bekah can go along the road a little way and keep him company.'

Mother looked reluctant as though she too would have liked to go along the road with Davy. She seemed about to say something but Father silenced her with a look.

'Excellent suggestion Father!' beamed Davy. 'Thank you for the parcel, Mother and for the food.

Wonderful!' He wrapped his arms around her and kissed her and her face lit up. 'I'll be back and see you soon, if I can. God' s peace and blessings on you all. Right, Come along Bekah.' Off they went. Bekah hadn't said a word. She didn't need to. Her face was radiant with happiness.

Mother stood for a moment, watching them until they were out of sight. Then she snatched Davy's dishes from the table and made much fuss about clearing up. 'Right girl, stop gawping and get on with your work!' she snapped at me.

Listen. *'Boys and girls grew up together. We went to school together and spent our spare time together. We were friends with many before we found the one we wanted to settle down with. We were in no hurry to marry or have babies. We had too many things we wanted to do, places to see.'*

Chapter 28

Curfew

The beach and all the shoreline were put out of bounds. So was nearly everywhere else if you were a girl. The Elders announced this in church the night after Davy came home. The Engineers were patrolling the coastline facing out to the rigs and the threat from the East. The island men and their new guns were patrolling the rest. Otherwise all villagers had to be in their homes by sundown and no women were to go more than half a mile out of the village unaccompanied.

'But how are we to gather the plants we need for dyeing wool or medicine?' asked Fin's sister, Hepzibah, braver than the rest. 'Or visit folk outside the village? Or go after a stray sheep?'

'You will have to take a male relation with you,' said the Chief Elder. 'If not your husband, or father then a brother or a son.'

'But what if our sons are children? What use are they?'

'A male relation over 12 years old will be deemed suitable,' said the Chief Elder.

The young boys preened themselves, already puffed up with the thought of power over older sisters and even their mothers. The women looked baffled. How could they stop us going freely about our business?

'What about the willow tree?' muttered Lowri. 'How can I just go and get some bark but must wait for Bryn to go too. It would be half a day away from work for him. This is madness.'

'These are dangerous times,' said the Chief Elder and, perfectly timed in the distance, even above the noise of the rising wind, we heard an explosion and the sound of shooting. Mothers gathered their small children closer to them. They all stood closer to their menfolk. .'Right,' said Father doing a head count, 'Amity, Lowri, Elspeth, Iolo, Bryn…'

As we walked home, huddled close together, I already had questions for Father. 'How can they stop us going about our business?' I asked. 'What if Dr John should send for Lowri? Won't I be able to go unless I take Bryn with me? Bryn has work to do. How can he? Oh it's such *a stupid* idea!'

'Hush child' said Father, looking around in case Mother had heard my questions. 'It seems harsh but the Elders have their reasons. These are difficult times. We want our womenfolk safe around us.'

'What of Davy?' asked Mother anxiously looking out to sea. 'Pray God that he will be alright.'

Many of the women I could see were clinging closer to their menfolk. Susannah was hanging tight on to Euan's arm, even though she had a toddler by the hand, the older boy trailing by her skirts and her baby wrapped in a shawl around her. It was as if suddenly we had become helpless.

But as I stomped angrily home ahead of my family, my heart still danced around the cave with Lucas and his music. I felt his arms around me and felt the lilting notes of the song he sang float through my body and down to my toes. His smile filled my head. The way he laughed when we understood each other, how we hardly needed words but our thoughts and feelings leapt from one to the other.

For two years I'd kept Fin in my heart. I'd had no one to share things with, no one to laugh with the way I'd laughed with him. But he had been so cold and distant since he returned that he'd made my heart cold too, as though a part of me had died. Now Lucas was making me feel alive again. It was wonderful and scary at the same time. I had to get back to Lucas soon. I needed to talk to him. And see him smile, and maybe dance…

I remembered, too, Davy's description of the village where music wasn't a sin or a crime but drifted and swirled through the air like smoke. Just the thought of it sent my feet tapping. The women in that village had a voice. They were equal to the men. It had been like that here once, according to Shenavar. How had we let it change? Those women would never allow themselves to be supervised by a twelve year old boy. Neither would I, I vowed.

And all the time those half-remembered English baby rhymes drifted around my head. Someone must have sung them to me long ago. Before I came to my parents' house someone, somewhere, sang to me in English. Maybe even before I came to the island. Could that be possible? Father said I came at the same time as the traders. Maybe they really had brought me. But from where? And why? Only Shenavar knew the whole story and now she was dead, I would never know.

But it made sense. No wonder I longed to get away from the island. It wasn't really my home. It was the only home I'd ever known and yet I'd also known somehow that it wasn't mine. I didn't belong here. *I didn't belong!*

It was a scary idea. Like when the sea washes away the sand from under you. Everything I'd known was wrong. But it was exciting too. It explained so much. If only I could have talked more to Shenavar. If only I could make sense of her notebooks. Maybe the secret was explained there. I needed to talk to Lucas too. I thought of the smile that lit up his face and even though he wasn't there, I smiled back at him.

'Amity!' my mother's voice crashed into my thoughts. 'Only you could find the thought of war amusing. Stop dawdling, girl. The sooner we're all home, the happier I'll be.'

I tried to look blank as we walked briskly along the path to home.

Lucas wouldn't get away tonight that's for sure. The wind was strengthening now and would be whipping up the waves in a sea channel already dangerous. He would be forced to wait, knowing what was going on and helpless to do anything about it. Father went out late on patrol, lantern in hand, gun over his shoulder. 'Mind, Callum, Bryn,' he said as stood on the threshold, 'Take care of the women and children.'

'We will, sir,' said Callum, almost saluting.

Elspeth shivered and slid closer to Bryn on the settle.

And what of Fin?

As I lay in bed listening to the wind howling down the chimney and the rain crashing against the windows I heard hoof beats galloping through the village. Not one of our clod hopping work horses, not even the small ponies that Davy had used on patrol. No this was clearly a high, long legged creature. I imagined Fin riding through night and wind and rain to do battle on behalf of the island. Despite his coldness, I still so much wanted him to be safe.

I went to sleep with Lucas's music dancing through my mind. But my dreams muddled thoughts of Fin on his horse. I still dreamed that I jumped from the rock, only this time I sprang up and danced to the music and didn't know whose arms had caught me.

Listen. *'One when we were searching through abandoned houses for anything we could use, we found a box with over £100,000 in it! That was a tremendous amount of money. I was so excited. Then I realised it was worthless, absolutely worthless, just paper and not even good enough to write on…'*

Chapter 29

Muddied and Muddled

'**D**on't be long!' Bryn said to me loftily, caught up in his new power as guardian of the womenfolk. 'Don't go more than half a mile from home. And mind you still have a batch of oatcakes to make!' This was my little brother talking. He barely came up to my shoulder and yet now, thanks to the Elders, he thought he could tell me what to do.

'I shall be as long as it takes,' I said, picking up my collecting bag and marching out of the door. 'And just remember, I had to feed you when you didn't even know what a spoon was for - and clean your dirty backside, so, whatever the Elders say, don't tell me what to do.'

Dear God, I wondered, could I last in this way of life until the traders returned and I could escape with them? I tried to put out of my mind the thought of going with Lucas. How could I? I was now convinced that, for some reason, known only to Shenavar, the traders had brought me to the island. It was only right, then, that they should take me away. I just had to keep going until they came back then maybe if Lucas got away, I could follow after and find him.

In the meantime, I refused to be a prisoner in my own home, guarded over by my little brother. Anyway, I had to see Lucas. I needed to know if he was all right. Yes, of course, I wanted to see him smile at me in the way he did. I wanted to feel his arms around me, however wicked that was. I longed for the magic again, that glimpse into another world. And for him.

Now the strange silence was telling me I was a good distance from the village. I'd come a different way down to the shoreline, then doubled back another way down to the beach from a different direction. This route took me past the Bone Pit where no villager liked to go. In the hungry years when there were too many people dying and not enough people with the strength to bury them properly, they had buried the bodies all together in one mass grave. Long ago people had built a low wall around it, and kept it decent. But no one went near it if they could help it.

Beyond the bone pit, the approach was difficult, boggy and marshy. Sometimes the mud was a few inches deep, other times nearly a metre or more. My legs and skirt were covered with mud, the weight dragging my skirt down. I wished I could just take it off and go on in my underwear and bare legs, but what if I didn't find my skirt again? So I slid and slithered on, grabbing tussocks of grass from the bank above me to keep myself steady, ignoring the cuts and scratches on my hands.

Arrgghh! There was a loud explosion from the direction of the sea. Bright yellow lights shot across the grey early summer sky, I missed my footing and sank gloopily over my knees.

I hoped Lucas had got away by now – but at the same time I hoped he hadn't, so I could see him just one more time. If not, he was trapped in the cave. Shelter would have become a prison. There were patrols along the shore, from sea and land. He wouldn't be able to forage for food. Even if he did catch a fish or trap a rabbit, he wouldn't be able to light a fire to cook it. Much too risky.

More gunfire over the sea. My heart thudded as I crawled off the boggy path on my hands and knees through the gorse and round the edge of the cliff. At last I dropped down onto the otter beach and scuttled into the cave. No sign of Lucas. Maybe he'd got away. Oh how I hoped he had. Oh, how I hoped he hadn't.

No. The rowing boat was pulled right up to the back of the cave. It was partly hidden by sand and seaweed and bird feathers so that anyone taking a quick glance in wouldn't see it. I looked around for the for the *sat.com* box on the ledge, under the blanket and another heap of pebbles. Lucas was somewhere around, I was sure. Softly, I called his name.

No answer. No gleam of long blonde hair. No flashing smile. No arms to hold me.

The cave seemed damp and bleak. Had we really danced there? I tried to remember the music Lucas had sung, imagined his arms around me, tapped my feet, trying to bring back the warmth and magic of the memory. There was no time. I'd probably already been missed. Power was going to my little brother's head.

I left the food next to the pebbles by the *sat com* box and slid back out of the cave, along the beach and back up the boggy path. My heart was heavy with disappointment. I'd so much wanted to see Lucas. If I knew he'd got away maybe that would be better. But I just didn't know.

On the edge of the village I felt safe. It was permitted for me to be there, in daylight at least. But I looked down at myself. My skirt was covered in mud. My hands and arms were streaked with mud and blood and scratches. My face hadn't fared much better. I still had my knitting sheath on my hip but the knitting - socks, nothing exciting - was soaked in muddy water and I'd lost a needle, so I couldn't even look properly respectably busy as I walked. Quickly, I weaved my way down the narrow, overgrown path past the Bone Pit, along the backs of houses to Bekah's. If I could get to Bekah's house, I could clean myself up a bit before going home.

I was just going along the path when I could hear hoof beats somewhere near. Hoof beats. Trotting. Slowing. My heart lurched. The hoof beats stopped. I looked up.

Fifty yards away, where the narrow path met the track was a rider on a horse. Fin. He sat on his horse, the reins loose in his hands and stared down the path at me. He was too far away for me to see his expression but I was waiting for him to come down the path to berate me for being out, for the filthy state I was in, for being - well - just for being me, I guess.

But he didn't. For a moment he looked straight at me. Then he looked away quickly and rode off. I could hear the hoof beats disappearing into the distance, trotting, galloping - gone. I knew he'd seen me but why hadn't he said anything? Part of me was relieved. Part of me was bitterly disappointed. Here I was falling in love with Lucas but my heart still ached for Fin. It was all so weird. Everything was weird. Why did life have to be like this? I plunged down the path and didn't stop running until I got to Bekah's.

'Amity! What's happened? Have you had an accident? Or...' Bekah's normally sunny face looked alarmed as she threw her small fork into the pot and wiped her hands on her apron. 'You haven't been attacked, have you?'

'No, no' I said, anxious to reassure her, 'but I...had a fall... and I can't go home like this.'

'A fall?' She looked sceptical. And worried.

'Please Bekah, can you just help me clean up a bit?'

I could see she wanted to ask more questions but she poured some water from a kettle by the fire into a basin and helped me strip off my clothes. She was quick thinking and practical - I knew she would make a good wife for a doctor like Davy. As I washed off the mud and blood she rummaged around upstairs and came down with one of her skirts that was near enough the same colour as mine and near enough to fit me, though a bit short. She gave me a clean headscarf and apron and tried to brush as much of the mud as possible off my shawl. 'You can always say you dropped that in the beck,' she said. 'But how did you get into such a state?'

'Best not to know,' I said. 'Honestly, Bekah. But thanks so much.'

She was giving me that sort of look that shows she knows something's up. 'Do you really know what you're doing?' she asked. 'You've been so strange lately...'

'It's all right. I'll explain when I can, promise.' Oh I wished I could tell her. Since Fin came back and I found Lucas all there seemed to be was secrecy and lies. I felt I'd lost Lowri because of it and now I was losing Bekah too. But there was no one to talk to, no one I could explain things too. 'Bekah…' I started to say when the door opened and her grandfather stamped in.

'Oh, hello Amity,' he said as he hung his cap up on a hook. 'And how are things with you?'

'Fine thank you sir,' I said bobbing him a curtsey while Bekah hastily swept up all my muddy clothes and shoved them out of sight.

'It's late for you to be out on your own. I suppose now we've got these new rules I'd better walk you home as we have no other men in our household to do so. I think even the Elders would consider me a respectable enough escort.'

'Thank you, sir, but there's really no need.' I said.

'Of course there isn't. Only the Elders are getting hysterical. Goodness knows what your Shenavar would have to say about it all. Still, those are the rules now and we mustn't look for trouble, must we?' He took his cap off the hook again, settled it on his head and we set off up the village.

We'd only gone about fifty yards when Callum appeared. 'It's alright, sir. I'll take Amity home from here,' he said.

'Good lad. You're family after all,' said Bekah's grandfather and turned round back to home, a tall figure, slightly stooping now and walking carefully along the potholed path.

'Callum!' I said angrily, shaking myself free from Callum's arm. Why did he always have to get hold of me? 'I'm not a parcel to be handed from man to man as if I were incapable of getting home by myself.'

Once the old man was out of earshot Callum asked

angrily. 'Where have you been? I knew you weren't in the polytunnels, nor at the community centre.'

'I was out looking for mosses,' I said firmly.

'Then where are they?' snapped back Callum.

'I er..I left them with Bekah. They were just the colours she needed to finish a piece of work,' I improvised quickly. All right, I lied. I hadn't picked any mosses at all but I had really left the bag at Bekah's.

'Anyway,' I challenged, 'Why were you looking for me?'

'No reason. I just wanted to know where you were, that's all, that you were safe.'

'I was quite safe, thank you. I don't need anyone following me about. And absolutely not you. Get that clear!'

We marched home side by side in silence. My head swirled with thoughts of Lucas and Fin, Fin and Lucas.

Listen. *'We used to go halfway round the world for holidays. Can you imagine that? We would go to where there was sunshine, blue skies and beaches. Getting on a plane was commonplace, nothing special. But mostly wherever we went, the people we met were friendly, pleased to see us. I want the world to be like that again.'*

Chapter 30

Attack

'Look!' screamed Bryn. 'The sky's on fire!' His face glowed and his eyes flashed terror in the strange light as a huge ball of fire shot up into the sky and lit up the sea for miles around.

'What is it? What is it?' I heard myself shouting. My head filled with wild thoughts of Lucas. And Fin. They fought for space in my head. Where were they? Were they caught up this? I wanted to run down the hill and find out. Nutmeg whimpered and twined himself around my legs, then pawed the ground, barking furiously.

The ball of light exploded it the air. I covered my ears against the noise of it. The light went. A plume of thick smoke filled the sky. Beneath it in the swirling blackness a boat split in two, snapped like a toy. Both halves were swallowed up in an instant by churning waves. The air filled with roar of wind and waves and water.

'Dear God,' said Father, 'It's come to this at last...'

And now we were in the middle of war. High powered boats raced towards the island attacking the boats of Engineers trying to guard the rigs. Engineers on land and sea fought back. A big boat dipped and tipped through the mountainous waves and seemed to haul something or someone aboard then turned and sped off out to sea.

'The White Star boats have had enough for now,' said Father, 'But they'll be back. How long can we hold out without help, without allies?'

Again we were up by the derelict house. He and Bryn were fetching stone and I'd brought them food as we tried to pretend life was normal. All morning I'd been preparing food. At the community kitchens we'd been packing more food for the Engineers at their camp on the far side of the island. Lowri and I had made hundreds of oatcakes for the men. For the first time in my life there were mutterings about whether we had enough and how we must go carefully with the stocks we had.

'We must go,' said Father, his face grim. Grabbing the half-filled cart he started striding out for home, Nutmeg close to his heels. Callum was running up the track towards us. 'The White Star attacked the rigs! They've attacked one of our patrols but we've got one of their boats. We blew it out of the water!'

'We saw,' said Father shortly. He went in to the house, took two guns from the high hooks and handed one to Callum.

'Time to go,' he said.

'Dr John already sent for Lowri at the community centre,' said Mother, hugging baby Liam so hard you'd think she'd crush the life out of him. 'They're expecting wounded men. Oh husband, will Davy be all right? '

'That's out of our hands,' said Father. 'But you'd better go too Amity. They need cool heads and capable hands. Bryn, see to the animals and take care of your mother and the little ones.'

'Can't I come with you, Father?' pleaded Bryn. 'There's another gun and I can…'

'No!' Father snapped. 'You are to stay here. God help us, we cannot risk all of our lives.'

For a moment it was clear Bryn wanted to argue. Instead, he swallowed hard and said 'Yes Father, I understand.' Father nodded approval and then he and Callum, guns over their shoulders, strode out towards the shore. I ran to the community centre. Not even the Elders could call this frivolous breaking of the curfew.

Lowri was already with Dr John in the large room that was the island hospital, with some of the older women who served as nurses when needed. The room, rarely used and normally so peaceful and quiet was now full of movement and hushed noise as they prepared for what was to come. Bekah was there too, in the background, checking a cupboard full of dressings. Our bandages were mainly strips of old sheeting, beyond all other uses, boiled and rolled up.

We heard hoof beats, the light sound of a small pony. Then - thank God - Davy came striding in. Bekah's face lit up with love and relief. Davy beamed at her but was instantly business-like. 'There are six men on the way in a wagon. Concussion, bullet wounds and burns. We must get ready before they arrive.'

'There are beds ready,' said Dr John, who suddenly

195

seemed so old and frail now in contrast with Davy's energy and purpose.

They all scrubbed up. 'When you think you're ready, start again and scrub some more,' said Davy. 'Cleanliness is next to godliness,' In the absence of any strong drugs or disinfectants, that was a good start in a hospital.

The men arrived - boys really - scared and hurt. Dr John and Davy looked carefully at each one of them and gave instructions to the women on what to do in the way of dressings. Lowri helped Dr John set a badly broken leg. The young man screamed in pain until they gave him something to soothe him. I could see Lowri watching everything Dr John did, as if committing it to memory.

Meanwhile Davy carefully removed a bullet from the shoulder of a young man who held onto Bekah's hand so tightly it was a miracle he hadn't crushed all the bones. The older village women looked to my brother Davy for instructions. Fin wasn't the only one who had grown up in the years since they'd left home. My brother was now a man of authority.

Having no special skills but being willing and energetic, I fetched and carried, hot water, dressings, removed soiled clothes, brought water for the men to sip, buckets for them to throw up in. I'd just mopped up my fifth bucket of sick and scrubbed the floor for the umpteenth time, when Zillah Makepeace - the old lady who had started the dancing in the laundry that day - came up to me with a wicked smile.

'You'll be pleased to know,' she said 'that Mrs Chief Elder is holding a prayer meeting at her house. She feels this is her overwhelming duty and the best contribution she can make in these difficult times.

Although, of course,' Zillah grinned wickedly. 'She would rather be working here with us but she knows where her true duty lies.'

I looked down at the bucket full of sick that I was about to dispose of and just wished that Mrs Chief Elder were near. Zillah grinned again. So did I.

Eventually, as evening fell, all was done and calm again. Davy took one last look at each of his patients. 'God help us but there'll be more tomorrow,' he muttered.

I'd gathered up a bundle of blood-soaked clothes and dressings to be burned. There were sheets and overalls to be washed too. Davy and Dr John, Lowri and Bekah all took off their huge white aprons. I was piling them into a basket, dropped my own on top when I realised how tired I was. More women had arrived, chaperoned by one of the husbands, to say they would take over the nursing and the rest of us should go home and get some sleep. Dr John said he would nap in a small room at the back, to be on call if needed. 'You've done well, all of you,' he said to us. 'And Davy, I'm proud of you. You've turned into a good doctor.'

'Largely thanks to your early help and advice sir,' said Davy.

'But now you must be getting back to your unit,' said Dr John. 'The guns have been quiet, I think. Perhaps there'll be no more wounded. We must pray so.'

'I'll walk you home,' said Davy to Lowri, Bekah and me, as he whistled up his little pony from where it had been cropping the short grass. As we all walked along, I thought of that night I'd ridden up on a high horse behind Fin. Had that really happened? Now we were all dog tired. My legs felt almost too heavy to lift as we made our way down the track.

Lowri and I lagged behind a little to give Bekah and Davy some small privacy. But they idled barely a moment outside Bekah's house, though her face looked happy enough as she turned and waved goodnight to us. At the end of the path to our house Davy briefly embraced Lowri and me. 'Thank you for your help today' he said. 'I'm blessed to have such sisters. And blessed again that you have a friend like Bekah. Send Mother my respects and apologies. I must get back to camp. I fear for what I might find there.' Then he mounted the pony and trotted off into the night.

Lowri and I were exhausted but sleep would have to wait. Our house was full of noise. Baby Liam was screaming with earache. Mother was rocking him by the fire and trying to soothe him. But as she walked up and down in the candlelight, her soothing words completely drowned out by his frantic, desperate screams she seemed strangely happy, and smiling. Probably because Davy was nearby and alive and well I supposed.

'He's fine, Mother,' Lowri reassured her. 'When he's in the hospital looking after the wounded, he's not in the fighting so is safe for now. And he's become so knowledgeable - everyone looks at him to know what to do. Even Dr John.'

Mother, still soothing a screaming Liam, beamed with pride.

'Is his ear still giving him pain?' asked Lowri. 'I have something in the still room that might help.'

'Good child,' said Mother, over the wails. 'And

then we have some news for you.'

Upstairs was another wail - Erin had woken now and was sobbing pitifully. 'I'll go to her,' I said to Mother and so I didn't notice the conversation between Lowri and Father and the buzz of excitement afterwards. It was a little while before Erin went back to sleep. One of Shenavar's stories eventually settled her. So I was surprised when I finally crept into our bedroom to find Lowri still awake and waiting for me, eager to talk.

'Cornelius was on patrol with Father!' she said. 'And as they waited they talked and…' her voice was an excited squeak '… and Cornelius has asked to marry me!' She sat up on the edge of the bed, her eyes shining in the flickering candlelight. 'Father said yes, if I was happy with that. He's to come tomorrow to get my answer! Oh Amity. I'm to be married and to Cornelius!'

I flung my arms around her. 'That's wonderful Lowri, wonderful. Cornelius is a lovely lad and you and he were made for each other.' I could feel Lowri's happiness radiating off her.

'And it's to be soon,' said Lowri, 'Cornelius and his brothers have been working on that little row of cottages beyond the crossroads, in readiness for the time when they set up on their own. One is almost ready. It has three bedrooms and a good garden and….oh Amity I'm so excited!' She gasped and stopped. 'Please God, let the fighting be over quickly. Please don't let there be a war now. Not now …not…'

'Not when you and Cornelius are about to be married and live happily ever after?' I teased.

'Is it so wrong to think so?' she asked, her face pale in the candlelight.

'No,' I laughed. 'If every young man were about to be married and thought more of love than of killing, then we'd soon run out of soldiers. And so wars. And wouldn't that be a good thing?'

'His parents will give us some furniture and Mother said we could have Shenavar's bed and some hens. Already there are fruit bushes in the garden that are beginning to grow. And Father will give us a blanket and they just have to clear the fireplace and make the chimney ready. And the brothers are clearing the garden and we shall try onions and potatoes. And Mother has kept some material so I shall have a new dress for the wedding. And...' She chattered into the night until the tiny stub of candle burnt out and we both eventually fell asleep, her head full of Cornelius and a wedding and a new home. And mine just full of muddle.

Listen. *'Before the wars we were free and independent. We had our own lives and didn't need to get married. But oh, when you met someone and knew you wanted to spend the rest of your lives together, that made it even more special.'*

Chapter 31

Broken Promises

'What news?' I asked, hurrying up the hospital path to where Engineers were bringing in more wounded. 'Two more with gunshot wounds,' said one. 'A parting shot from a White Star boat.'

The young man on the stretcher was gasping in pain, his jacket soaked with blood. I rushed to open the doors for the stretcher party and guide them to the hospital room. 'Any news from the patrols?' I asked the stretcher-bearer, as he placed the wounded man as gently as he could onto a table bleached white with scrubbing. 'Any news from the shore?'

'No' he said looking surprised. 'Nothing there. The patrols are just to fool the White Star boats that we've got a big army. But,' he said bitterly, 'I don't think they're that stupid. Right, sir,' he said to Davy, 'There's another one to bring in, losing blood, but not as fast as this one.'

Davy was already snipping away at the man's

blood-soaked jacket. Dr John went out to meet the other wounded man. Lowri went with him, brisk and business like but even so I could see the excitement of her imminent marriage all over her. She couldn't help the spring in her step or the sparkle in her eye.

'Come on,' said Fortitude Andrews, one of the older nurses. 'Amity, you can help me see to the other young lads.'

While Fortitude changed dressings, I cleaned up, mopped floors, fetched more bandages, brought the men drinks, sorted out more sheets and aprons to be washed. There was plenty to do and I was glad of it as it helped dim the noise and worry of the thoughts in my head.

Then suddenly... You know that feeling you have when you just know someone is looking at you?

I was in a tiny room, not much more than a cupboard really, with my back to the ward. I was bundling a heap of blood-stained sheets into the basket, while singing in my head the song that Lucas had sung, the song we'd danced to. Then I had that feeling of eyes willing me to turn round. I wanted to whip round and see who was staring at me but I made myself wait. I folded the sheet then slowly I picked up the basket, balancing it on my hip and turned round.

Fin was standing there. He was at the far end of the ward, a piece of paper in his hand. He'd been talking to Dr John and one of the wounded Engineers. Dr John was talking to one of the women and Fin was just standing there, not looking at the piece of paper, not looking at the wounded man - but looking at me. Along the length of the ward his eyes fixed on mine. The look made my heart turn over.

Despite his black suit, cropped hair and the new

weariness on his face, he was gazing at me the way he used to, when we lay in the sand at otter rocks, his eyes full of love and laughter. *This* wasn't Fin, member of the Elect, preacher and leader of the Engineers. This was the boy I'd fallen in love with and the boy who loved me, the boy who made me a promise. Our eyes locked and for a moment he seemed to move towards me. Then Dr John turned back to talk to him. Fin took his eyes away from me and the moment was over.

I had to speak to him. There was so much I needed to know.

I was still standing there, clutching the laundry basket when there was a small commotion at the doorway to the ward. Mr and Mrs Chief Elder had arrived. They processed down the ward talking to the men and then conducted a short prayer service. Well, *short* by the Chief Elder's standards. His voice droned on. And on. Until finally Dr John gave a small cough and one of the men gave a terrifying groan. The Chief Elder brought the prayers to a quick conclusion. I darted out of the ward. But I still hadn't escaped. Mrs Chief Elder was heading towards me.

'Ah, Amity,' the smile on her face like the gleam on a worm-rotten apple. 'Chastity Llewellyn is not well. She is *so* devout and *such* a good worker, anxious to do the Lord's work on Earth and bring up her children in the ways of righteousness.'

Chastity had half a dozen children all under seven years old, the sort who always cried - apart from the younger set of twins who just screamed. No wonder Chastity was unwell.

'So I told her that you will be pleased and proud to look after her children until she recovers. No work is too humble in the service of the Lord.'

'But..' I said pointing to the overflowing washing basket, which was pretty humble already I thought.

Her face wrinkled in disgust. 'As soon as you've done that. She's expecting you. Run along.'

I shrugged and picked up the basket and marched off to the laundry determined to talk to Fin as soon as I could. I didn't have to wait long. As I turned into the long corridor that led from the laundry, I saw Fin striding along away from me.

'Fin!'

He turned and stopped. There was no one else around. Remembering the way he'd looked at me just a short while before, I walked quickly towards him. I'd forgotten the hurt of the way he'd ignored me since he'd been back. I'd forgotten the way he'd looked through me as if I was lower than the low. I'd forgotten the way he'd spoken to me in my parents' kitchen. All I remembered was the look in his eyes as he'd gazed at me across the hospital room. I was nervous but smiling as I hurried towards him.

He stared at me. 'Amity, shouldn't you be looking after Chastity Llewellyn's children?' he asked.

'Oh yes, I shall, but I had to talk to you first. Fin..'

'Then please be quick as I have a lot to do. I have to be back at camp.'

What was I meant to make of this? I hesitated.

'Amity, I know we were friendly when we were children. But that was a long time ago. When I was a child I spake like a child, thought like a child. Now, Amity, the time has come to put away childish things. Do you understand?'

'Oh yes, Fin, I understand, all too clearly' I said, wondering how on earth I could have imagined a look of love.

'No you don't Amity,' he said. His shoulders sagged. 'You've no idea.' He looked bone weary. He looked away down the corridor as though trying to gather his thoughts. When he looked at me, his eyes seemed exhausted but honest and open, eyes I recognised.

'I'm sorry, Amity, sorrier than you can know.'

I wasn't expecting that.

'You were, are, very precious to me. And if things were different...' He reached out as if to touch me, hold me. Then he shook his head. 'I made you a promise that I cannot keep.' His eyes flashed 'Though I wish it were otherwise! Oh how I wish it. But circumstances are changed and I have work to do, responsibilities I cannot share. I'm answerable to other people not just myself. The time is not right for us, nor never will be.'

He looked into my eyes and all I could see was sadness. And that was the moment I knew it really was all over for us. Whatever the reasons for the change in Fin, I could see it wasn't easy for him and that I was making it harder, just by being there. I wanted to argue, to cry, maybe even plead but I knew for absolute certain it would be pointless. So instead I took a huge breath and tried to be calm and dignified and hoped he couldn't hear my heart thudding. I thought of the little carved otter I'd kept for two years and was glad that I'd flung it into the waves.

'We were very young when you made your promise, not much more than children,' I said. 'Much too young for it to be binding.'

'Oh Amity! You can even understand that. If only...' For a split second he looked agonised but then got himself under control. 'Our lives are different now. You must get on with yours. I have work to do. You must please, forget about me. It is better that way.'

The silence and the sadness hung heavy in the air. I had so much I wanted to ask him but the words died in my throat. We stood there for some minutes, saying nothing but unable to walk away.

Finally Fin spoke, the sadness in his eyes replaced by that now-familiar chill. 'Now I must get on,' he said briskly. 'I have no time for idle chat. You too have work. I will not detain you.'

I pulled myself up to the greatest height I could muster and, despite the laundry basket balanced on my hip, tried to look as dignified as possible. I looked him straight in the eyes. 'Don't worry. I won't bother you again.'

'Good. That's for the best.' He nodded and turned to go. Then immediately turned back. 'Just be careful, Amity,' he said quietly. 'You must take your chances but please, be careful.' And he was gone.

I watched him disappear. There was no future for the two of us, just a broken promise. I knew somehow, in a strange way, he still cared for me, but clearly, not enough. And what did he mean about taking my chances? It was as if he knew I was planning to go.

Then when I was leaving the hospital I saw Fin again. This time he was talking to Mr and Mrs Chief Elder - and Priscilla. She was standing between her grandparents looking pretty and neat and obedient and humble and all the things I'm not. It was obvious that the Chief Elder was inviting Fin in to his house. Fin refused. Then he looked at Priscilla and seemed to hesitate. Mrs Chief Elder asked him again and then all four of them walked up the steps into the Chief Elder's house. Fin held the door open and smiled down at Priscilla while Mrs Chief Elder beamed smugly.

So that was the way of it. Fin and Priscilla. Those were the people he was answerable to. They were the responsibilities he couldn't share.

So much for thinking he still cared for me.

Listen. *'My first proper boyfriend gave me a silver bracelet for my birthday. I loved it as I loved him. Even when we no longer loved each other I wore the bracelet because of the love there had been.'*

Chapter 32

Reflection

The needle-sharp cold drizzle found its way through every gap of my clothes, down my neck, in my eyes and chilled me to the very bone. I didn't care. I wrapped my shawl around me, drew my feet under my wet skirt to stop them freezing further and stared down at the island from the shelter of the graveyard wall.

I hadn't yet gone to Chastity Llewellyn's house. She and her tribe of terrible children could wait, whatever Mrs Chief Elder said. I needed to think. Talking to Fin hadn't told me anything, just given me more unanswerable questions. What did he mean that I had to take my chances? Why was he telling me to be careful? What did he know?

But Fin and Priscilla. *Priscilla!* The thought was so ridiculous it almost made me laugh, despite the icy rain. But it explained a lot. How that boy had changed. I didn't know him at all any more. The sooner I got him out of my head - and my heart - the better. Then there was Lucas... I longed to go down to the shore. Was Lucas safe? Had he made his escape? Or - and I tried not to think it - had he been shot or wounded again? I needed to know. But the shoreline was too dangerous for so many reasons, so I'd fled up here instead.

Despite the attacks by the White Star boats, other people were getting on with their lives. Lowri and Cornelius, obviously. They would be married within weeks. By this time next year they'd probably have a baby. Their lives would be complete with each other. Then how would she be able to help Dr John?

Maybe there'd be no need. Dr John now seemed so old that it was clear he couldn't carry on alone for much longer. Now Davy was back he would surely stay when the Engineers left. He and Bekah would be married too. So my best friend and my sister, the last of our age to be married, were within weeks of being settled. No doubt Fin would soon be paired off with Priscilla. How Mrs Chief Elder would love that.

And what about me? What would I do? I was stuck. Not just stuck on the island but stuck at home with a mother who seemed determined to make my life wretched. Even Shenavar had abandoned me. Only Lucas seemed to care. Even though I was horribly uncomfortable, I could feel myself drifting off into a little dream about Lucas. Right now he was the only worthwhile thing in my life. Had he really asked me to go with him?

The rain stung my face as I peered down on the island, at the creaking wind turbines, the peaty smoke from house fires. On the far cliffs I could see the Engineers' camp, tents set up in the ruins of the old air force base. Below me was the community centre and hospital and the big polytunnels with their tattered, much repaired covering. Between them small figures scuttled, heads down in the rain. Sheep chomped at the patches of sheltered grass that had survived the oil storm. A group of men strode purposefully along the path leading down to the shore. The island men on patrol. Please let them not find Lucas…

The sea was choppy but quiet. One of the Engineers' boats bounced along the waves between the shore and the oil rig. Getting away with Lucas was surely a dream. But maybe I could get away with the Engineers. There must be a way I could smuggle myself onto one of the trucks. There were villages on Mainland where I could make a life, surely? It had to be better than here.

What was that? For a moment I thought I'd seen a tiny dot on the horizon. A tiny black dot way out to sea. I stared through the rain dripping from my hair and eyelashes. No. Nothing. The White Star boats had raced off to the north east, but this speck was in the completely opposite direction, way down to the south west.

I peered again. No. I must have imagined it.

I was soaked through now. I wrapped my wet shawl around me and got to me feet and took one last look at the island beneath me. It wasn't my land. It wasn't my home. I didn't belong here. Maybe I never had. Where had I come from? Why had Shenavar brought me here? Now I was trapped.

I ran down the hill, sliding on the wet grass. When the traders came again I would leave with them. I just had to keep my courage until then.

Listen. '*You can plot and plan as much as you like but sometimes decisions make themselves.*'

Chapter 33

Marriage Plans

Father's face was stern in the firelight.

It was late when I got home. I'd finally gone to see to the terrible Llewellyn children and helped their mother, who didn't seem all that ill to me and who just moaned all the time. But what do you expect from a friend of Mrs Chief Elder?

The not-belonging feeling was still with me as I walked in to the house. The evening had gone on without me. Mother was upstairs murmuring to one of the little ones. Callum was out on patrol. Everyone else was in bed. There was no one to greet me except Father and even he didn't seem particularly pleased to see me. 'So you finally went to Chastity Llewellyn's house, did you?' he said as I took off my still-wet shawl and spread it out to dry near the fire.

'Of course,' I replied.

'Then why were you seen scampering about on the hillside?' he demanded. 'Why is it wherever I go someone tells me that they've seen you wandering on your own? You flit around the island as if you have no cares, no responsibilities, no duties. Don't think you haven't been seen. Have you no sense at all of what's fitting?'

'That's unfair! I work hard. I do my share, more...'

'Quiet!' He slammed his hands down on the arms of the chair.

I dropped my eyes and stood very still. Father had never before been like this with me.

'Other girls of your age are married with children to keep them busy. Even your little sister Lowri will be married soon. Yet you... you seem to live in some perpetual fairyland when you think you can please yourself when you come or go or do any work. It's gone on long enough.'

I glanced up at him. His face was like stone. I looked down again.

'I don't say you don't work hard. You've always been a worker. But you could never be like the other girls, could you? Always wanting more, always wanting to be somewhere else. Once I could say oh yes, that you devoted to much time to Shenavar, that you were a good girl. And you were.' His voice softened then but not much. He took a deep breath. Now his voice came out like ice. 'This can't go on. You're not a child any more. It's time you were married, with a husband to care for and children of your own to stop you from gallivanting round the countryside. That's why...'

He hesitated and I looked up and I wondered what on earth he was going to say.

'...that's why you will marry Callum.'

'Callum!' This can't be right. I can't have heard. He

couldn't mean it. The words wouldn't fit into my head and I struggled to work them out.

'You can't really mean I'm to marry Callum? Callum!'

My brain might have struggled to grasp what he said. But my body realised straight away and my insides heaved to prove it. The thought of marriage to Callum made me feel so sick that for a moment I thought I would throw up there and then in front of the fire.

Now Father was talking very quickly, as if he had something unpleasant to say and wanted to get it over with. At the same time, his voice was getting further and further away. I couldn't understand what he was saying.

'He has asked for you and I have said yes. He's a good match. He's kin to your mother. He's a skilled craftsman and a hard worker. He has kept his parents' house in good repair all the time he's been with us.'

'But...' I could hardly trust my voice. This all seemed so unreal.

'I know you might have had other thoughts.' Again Father's voice softened a fraction. 'That's why we didn't rush to marry you off when others came calling. Fin knows your ways and always seemed like part of the family already,' he said in a wondering sort of tone as if speaking to himself. The ice returned. 'But there are no hopes for you there. Even if Fin did retain feelings for you, the way you've been behaving in recent weeks will make you no suitable match for one of The Elect. Oh no. He will be looking elsewhere for a suitable match among the daughters of the elders.'

'Oh Father, I can't marry Callum! I just can't!'

'You can and you will,' said Father, banging the

arm of the chair again. 'You cannot go on the way you have. You have brought shame on us all and will only bring more if you carry on in the same fashion. Just be grateful that there's someone willing to make an honest woman of you. At least Callum can't say he doesn't know you well enough.' He paused. 'Your mother will set you up with what you need. There's nothing to stop you marrying as soon as possible. Next week perhaps. The sooner the better. I'll see the Chief Elder tomorrow. Then Lowri can wait a month or two for Cornelius.'

'But Father!'

'Enough! It is decided! You shall marry Callum!' He walked out of the room and I fell to my knees in front of the feeble warmth of the dying fire.

How long I lay there I don't know. But the candle had burned right down and the fire had gone out.

No. Callum would soon be back home from his patrol duties. I couldn't see him. I never wanted to see him! My skin crawled at the thought and I could feel myself going faint again but I scrambled to my feet. I had to do something. For if I didn't, by this time next week I would surely be married to Callum, living with him in his parents' old home a few miles away. Never!

My plan to escape with the Traders had vanished too. By the time they returned I could well be a mother or carrying Callum's baby. That thought made me sick again.

Deep breaths. Think. Breathe. Think. There was only one answer. 'Take your chances,' Fin had said.

I crept upstairs. Everyone was asleep. All I could hear was the gentle sounds of them breathing, the occasional snuffle from the babies, or a snore from

Bryn or Father. So Father could sleep. He had made me the most wretchedly unhappy girl on the island yet he could sleep soundly in his bed. No wonder I felt I didn't belong here.

In our room Lowri was smiling as she slept. Dreaming of Cornelius no doubt. Part of me wished she would wake up so I could tell her what had happened, explain what I had to do. But maybe it was better that she carried on sleeping and smiling.

After all my planning, I didn't take much. Just a bag with Shenavar's notebooks and the word book. I had my knitting sheath on my belt. I took Lowri's shawl. It was thicker and warmer than mine, and dry. She wouldn't mind. Downstairs I filled the bag with as much food as I could fit in it. By Lowri's still room I hesitated over the medicines, but they needed those in the hospital. I left them untouched. If I'd had pen and paper I would have left a note, to try and explain. But how could I? What would I say?

Then I slipped out of the door, carefully shutting it behind me. In the shed Nutmeg whimpered a bit but recognised it was me and went straight back to sleep.

This is the way I left the only family I had ever known.

Chapter 34

Danger

The wind had eased to a stiff breeze and the rain was no more than a persistent drizzle, so by island standards everything was eerily quiet as I slipped through the darkness and past the sleeping houses.

Would Lucas still be there? Or had he already got away? And what would I do then? I didn't care. I would think of that if I had to. All that mattered now was getting away from the island and especially away from Callum. Desperation drove me on. Now I was clear of the houses and would have to cross the open grassland at the end of the village. Even with so little moonlight I could be seen. I waited for a minute in the shelter of the ruined van with its faded sign for next day delivery.

My eyes strained. Over in the direction of the Engineers' camp I could see dim lights and sense some movement. They would be patrolling along the north east coast of the island where the cliffs had the best view point over the oil rigs and the open sea to the east. What of the island patrols, the band of armed men? That included Callum. I listened hard. Silence. All I could hear was the small whoosh of the wind and the gentle hiss of the drizzle. Above that, nothing. Wherever the island patrol was, it wasn't near here.

Now or never. Crouching low, clutching my bag close to me like a baby, I made it to the path down to the shore and the stepping stones, thanking God that I knew my way so well. The tide was high. Even on the stepping stones the water was way above my knees. But I had no time to be nervous, just stepped out, trusting my feet and my memory.

As I splashed through the water I wondered if I should have brought shoes. Would I need shoes where I was going? Where was I going? I jumped down from the rock and landed softly. The rowing boat was out of its hiding place and sitting on the sand. Lucas must still be here! Almost giddy with relief, I tiptoed to the cave entrance and stopped. How to let Lucas know I was here, that it was me and not the island men or the Engineers with their rifles? If I startled him, his instinct would surely be to attack. I remembered the sharpness of that knife.

'One, two, three, four five...' My voice wobbled and cracked. I hadn't realised how frightened I was. Even though I sang softly, under the shelter of the cliff, the noise would carry as far as it needed.

'Once I caught a fish alive...' A second's pause and the answering line came low and clear through the darkness.

'Six, seven, eight, nine ten...'

Lucas stepped out onto the sand and together we sang 'Then I let it go again.'

Despite the danger, we laughed and Lucas put his arm around me and hugged me, as if it was quite normal that I should turn up at the cave in the middle of the night. As if he'd been waiting for me.

As we slipped quickly into the shelter of the cave entrance I showed him my bag with what I'd brought with me and held his hand. Then I pointed to the rowing boat and mimed getting in and waving goodbye to the island.

Lucas frowned. 'Are you sure?' he asked and even though the words meant nothing I could tell what he was asking and nodded hard. He frowned again, uncertain. Then he asked me something that I didn't understand and I reached for Shenavar's word book which was silly because it was too dark to read it. He pointed to the sea and mimed rough waves as if warning me that it would be dangerous.

I laughed. I was so sure. It seemed the obvious, the only, thing to do. 'There's nothing left for me on the island. Nothing!' I said.

He looked into my eyes as if to be sure of what I was saying and that I really meant it. Then he too laughed and drew me into his arms and kissed me. Gently, first on one cheek, then the other. The last, only, boy who'd kissed me had been Fin more than two years ago. Soft and gentle, Lucas's lips barely touched my skin yet they were clearly a promise of more. I felt excited and safe all at once. Most importantly I knew I was doing the right thing.

Holding my hand, he led me into the cave, where the open *sat.com* box showed a screen with circles and a tiny dot of light bleeping very quietly. Lucas pointed out to sea. The dot of light was moving to the centre of the screen. I remembered the tiny dark shape I thought I'd seen far out to the south west that morning. Maybe it hadn't been my imagination.

'The rescue boat?' I asked. 'The boat to take you away?'

'Yes. It is near.' He nodded.

Then with the old blanket from my bed wrapped around our shoulders we sat and watched the tiny light moving ever closer. 'I can hear it! I whispered. 'Listen!'

Far away there was a very low noise. We could hardly hear it above the sounds of the sea but after a minute or so there was no doubt. An engine. Not far out to sea. The engine stopped.

'But it could be the Engineers! Or a White Star boat!' The alarm in my voice made my meaning clear.

Lucas shook his head and pointed to the dot, now at the very centre of the screen. He snapped the box shut. We were standing just inside the cave peering out into the blackness. The rocks, I thought, didn't they look different? Was there a low flat rock at the very edge, furthest from the shore? I tried to remember it in daylight. Surely it hadn't always been there? It was just a black shape in the darkness almost impossible to make out as I strained my eyes, until I saw something. 'It moved!' I whispered to Lucas. 'It moved. It must be the boat!' We grasped each other's hands tightly.

Then I heard something else - above us, further along the cliff. I froze as I listened. Stamping feet, muttered voices. The island patrol. Very quickly getting closer to us. The sound at first faint and far away now filled the night. They couldn't! We were so close to getting away! Why did they have to come now? Even in the darkness I could see the horror on

Lucas's face. He'd waited all this time. It mustn't go wrong at the very last moment. We could only wait, helpless, as the noise got nearer. 'Hey!' shouted a man somewhere up above us. 'There's something down there, by the rocks. Something moving!'

They'd seen us.

'It's a boat!' came another shout. 'You were right, Mac. That must be what you saw before!' 'Get it!' yelled a voice I recognised as Callum's. A sudden explosion made us jump and clutch each other. Gunshot cracked onto the rocks, sending up fierce little spurts of sea water.

'Callum you idiot!' a man shouted. 'They're out of range and you've wasted ammunition.'

'Come on!' shouted another. 'Let's get closer. There's a way down here isn't there?'

Now we could hear the man crashing down the cliff. Some were coming down the steep and boggy side and were sliding in the mud, getting caught on gorse and bushes. Others were making for the path on the other side of the rocks. Lucas and I pressed ourselves against the back of the cave wall, trying to disappear into the blackness, trying not to breathe.

The rowing boat! It was out there on the sand. The men would see it as soon as they got to the beach. Then they would hunt us down. Lucas looked desperately around the cave but he knew there was no other way out. We were trapped.

The beach would soon be full of armed men. Even if we made a dash for it and managed to get to the rowing boat, we'd never get it in the water. The men would shoot us first. One of the men had got past the mud and bushes and thorns and was clambering over the rocks towards the motor boat. What if he shot the men in the boat? Or sank it?

'Oh please don't kill our rescuers!' I prayed. The tide was high and still coming in. As the first man clambered cross the rocks in the darkness a wave washed over him and knocked him off his feet. He struggled for a while, his head under the water but then choking and gasping he managed to pull himself out and lay there, clinging to the rock.

'We can't get to it this way,' he shouted. 'We're better going back up and along!' Someone hauled him to his feet and they made their way back to the cliff.

Others of the patrol had got down the path on the other side of the rocks and were getting close. But they couldn't find the stepping stones. They were wading up to their chests in water and every wave knocked them.

Above us I heard a horse gallop then stop. A voice shouted. Fin!

Fin had eyes like a hawk. He would see the waiting motor boat and the little dinghy. He also knew where the stepping stones were. There was no hope now. Fin, the commander, Fin the hellfire preacher, Fin of the ice cold eyes would have no mercy.

I groaned. It was all over. Lucas would be recaptured. Just as I'd learned to love him, I would lose him. He mustn't die. He was brave and determined and wanting peace. It would be such a *waste!* Whether I was killed or not, or had to go back and marry Callum didn't matter. Either way, life ended here.

No! I tugged Lucas's hand. We had to make a dash for the boat. Better to die trying than be taken back to a life I loathed. Lucas didn't move. He was frowning as if trying to understand. Fin was shouting to the men.

'Get back up here!' Fin was yelling in a voice that demanded to be obeyed. 'Leave this to the Engineers! They have it in hand!'

A few men muttered. 'They're welcome to these gorse bushes,' said one as he clambered back up the bank.

'If they want to get soaked to the skin and knocked off their feet, they're welcome to that and all,' said another who was wading chest-high on the other side of the rocks. In a few minutes the men had scrambled back up to the cliff top.

'Get yourselves back to the village,' commanded Fin. 'Your duty is to keep your wives and families safe. Keep circling the village until the new patrol takes over at dawn.'

The men moved off. They were going away! Fin had sent them right away from us and his instructions meant they wouldn't be coming back. What was he playing at? I glanced towards the east. The tiniest, narrow slip of light was just appearing under the clouds. It would soon be daylight. The rescue boat couldn't wait any longer. This was our last chance!

I looked at Lucas and we nodded. We ran, hand in hand across the sand, hearts pounding, heads down, any minute expecting the sharp crack of bullets. Across the beach we grabbed the little rowing boat, I threw in my bag and pushed the boat out into the waves. Despite the high tide, the boat was scraping on the rocks. We had to keep pushing until we hit deep water.

We were soaked to the skin and could hardly see what we were doing. All the time I was waiting for the sound of gunshot, sure that someone would stop us. It was hard to control the little boat as it bobbed crazily between the rocks and the tide. Lucas could

use only one hand so it was mostly left to me to guide
it. Sometimes my heavy skirt kept catching on the
rocks. Other times it threatened to drag me right
down under the water. My bruised and bleeding legs
felt like cotton wool, but we had to keep going.

At last the water was deep enough. I clambered in
with a push from Lucas and then pulled him in after
me. The little boat rocked so much I thought it would
throw us right out again. But Lucas flung himself
down and spread the weight. With the single oar he
pushed us clear of the rocks. We bobbed in hopeless
circles for agonising minutes as he struggled to
control the boat and the oar. I leaned out trying to
paddle with my hand to get us straight, the muscles in
my arm and shoulder screaming out in pain. Finally
we set shakily on our course. I clutched the sides of
the little boat and looked back at the island, waiting
for gunfire.

Fin was standing alone on the beach. Just standing,
watching us go.

I wondered if the Engineers were waiting round
the other side of the point to capture the rescue boat
and us. Kill us all maybe. But I'd seen them go off in
the opposite direction on the top of the island. And
the island men were inland, circling the village out of
sight of the shore because Fin had ordered them to…
I couldn't make sense of it but was just relieved to
still be alive.

Now Fin moved. He must have seen something
lying on the beach. He bent down, picked it up and
brushed the sand off it. It was hard to see in grey light
of dawn, but he seemed almost to be laughing. Then
whatever it was, he whipped his arm back and threw
it hard towards our little boat. Instinctively, I put out

my hand and caught it - which made the boat rock even more wildly.

I looked at what I'd caught. A small piece of wood, battered and bashed and bleached by its time in the sea, but still recognisable - the otter that Fin had carved as a symbol of his promise to me. I'd thrown it in the sea and the sea had sent it back for Fin to give to me again. It fitted into my hand as if it had never left. As our little dinghy dipped and bobbed around the rocky point my last sight of Fin was him standing on the beach, arm raised as if wishing us God Speed.

Our rescuers hauled us aboard the motor boat and wrapped us in blankets. Within seconds we were roaring off in the chilly grey dawn. As Lucas and our rescuers talked in rapid English, I shivered as I watched the island disappear from view.

I'd done it! I'd finally left the island and all it represented. And I'd escaped Callum. I had no idea what was going to happen next but I was heading for a new world, a world with colour and music and freedom, a new life, a different future, with Lucas.

But in my pocket my frozen fingers still stroked the familiar shape of the little carved otter that Fin had given me twice.

The End

About the Author

Sharon Griffiths was born and brought up in Wales. She read English at the University of Bristol and has since worked as a journalist, first for the BBC, then ITV. She now writes regular opinion columns for a number of newspapers. *Amity and the Angel* is her third published novel.

She is married to fellow journalist Mike Amos and they live in a house full of words.

Other books by Sharon Griffiths:

The Accidental Time Traveller (Avon 2008)

A wonderfully warm romantic comedy - The Bookseller

Sharon is a master storyteller. The plot twists keep you hooked until the very last page - Eastern Daily Press

The Lost Guide to Life and Love (Avon 2009)

An excellent read - OK magazine

Well written with believable, empathetic characters and a satisfying plot – the story zips along - Daily Mail

Acknowledgements

Many thanks to Wendy Robertson and Avril Joy of Damselfly for their professionalism, encouragement and enthusiasm.

And to Mike Amos, Adam and Stacey, Owen and Sam for making life fun.

Printed in Great Britain
by Amazon